UNNATURAL DISASTERS

EDITED BY
DANIEL PYLE

BLOOD BROTHERS PUBLISHING
2011

Blood Brothers Publishing

www.bloodbrotherspublishing.com

ISBN: 978-0-615-56512-5

Printed in the United States of America

Cover Artwork Copyright © 2011 by Enoch Pyle

1 3 5 7 9 10 8 6 4 2

For Jeremiah Pyle,
with whom I experienced at least one natural disaster.
More if you count hellish Missouri summers.

For Jeremiah Pyle,
with whom I experienced at least one natural disaster.
More if you count hellish Missouri summers.

CONTENTS

39 DAYS

ROBERT J. DUPERRE

AUGUST 18TH

Waves crashed against the side of the building. To Angela it sounded like the rocky coast of Maine. She leaned over the side of the roof and glanced down. The water smacked against the building again and flowed around it. She swore she could see formless black splotches beneath the surface and immediately imagined a capsized oil tanker dumping gallon after gallon of crude into the ocean.

"How high is it now?" asked Tommy.

She furrowed her brow and counted the windows above the water line. "Fourth floor," she said, "almost to the fifth."

"Shit. That's higher than yesterday."

A stout wind hit her from the rear, momentarily lifting her knees from the concrete. Her hair stood straight out, hovering over the angry sea below. With a yelp she gripped tight to the railing and spun around, wedging her butt in the crook between the partition and the floor. Tommy hurried over to her, eyes wide with panic.

"You okay?" he asked.

Angela nodded.

Tommy slumped beside her. The wind died down. He crawled to the center of the roof, rummaged through his backpack, and brought back a handful of snacks.

"You hungry?"

"Sure."

They sat there together, munching on Nilla Wafers and staring at the gray and ominous sky. A few drops of rain began to fall.

They burned.

AUGUST 20TH

A helicopter soared overhead. It landed on the building three down from where Angela and Tommy had been trapped. The few people on the roof rushed it, and men in fatigues ushered them aboard. The helicopter rose again and disappeared over the horizon.

"How many's that now?" asked Angela.

"Fifteen over the last week," Tommy replied. "Looks like they're working their way toward us. Might only be a few days till it's our turn."

Angela grunted. "Good. I'm getting tired of sitting around doing nothing."

She stood up and cracked her back. For the first time in a week the sun poked its warming face through the clouds. She bathed in its heat and spread out her arms. Lesions covered her skin, the result of not getting into the complex in time when the poisoned rains fell. Even their tent hadn't been spared—its canvas hide was peppered with black marks and tiny holes. It was better than nothing, however. A headache spiked behind her eyes. She crawled inside.

The interior of the tent was hot, and she found it hard to breathe. She tried to get comfortable, flapping her sleeping bag in an attempt to alleviate the humidity that had gathered in the cloth cocoon. Nothing seemed to help. It was still hotter than hell.

With a sigh she crawled back out of the tent, towing the

sleeping bag behind her, and spread it out on the roof. She lay down on it and curled into a ball, squeezing her eyes shut against the intense brightness of the outside world. She felt Tommy kneel beside her.

"You want some company?" he asked.

Angela grunted in affirmation.

Tommy slid in behind her and wrapped his arm around her midsection. He wedged his forearm into the underside of her breasts. She felt his breath against the back of her neck while her skin tingled under the sun's rays.

For the first time since the whole mess started Angela smiled and allowed the sound of the crashing waves to usher her off to sleep.

AUGUST 25TH

It had been four days since the last chopper came around, and Angela had started to get nervous. At least the sun had stayed out. It made the days scorching, especially on the roof's harsh concrete, but by the middle of the night, when the air cooled to almost arctic temperatures, she wished for the heat to return. *Damned either way*, she thought.

She made her way to the edge of the roof and gazed across the watery landscape. Hartford had become one with the ocean. That ocean rose every day, approaching their sanctuary with ever-greedy fingers. Luckily for her and Tommy, they lived in one of the taller apartment complexes on the east end of the city. The water was still a good sixty feet from overtaking them. That gave them time, at least.

But that time was running out.

"Yo, Ang!" a faint voice called out to her.

She turned around. On the roof of the apartment building to the west stood Rachid and Roberta Freeman, surrounded by their four children and Dexter McCutchens.

They waved at her and held up a handwritten sign. *Want to play a game?* it read.

Tommy chuckled from behind her. "Checkers again?" he asked.

Angela bent over, grabbed the wax board they'd been using to communicate with those stranded on the other roof for the last couple of weeks, and scribbled *Sure thing, your move* in large letters. She held it up, and little Jermaine Freeman clapped. Even from a distance, she could see the whites of their teeth as they smiled.

They played for a few hours, until the sun began dipping over the horizon. When it became impossible to see, Angela and Tommy simply packed up their cheap checkerboard and tossed it into the tent.

"See you tomorrow!" screamed Tommy. They could barely hear when their far-away friends returned the sentiment.

They crawled into their sleeping bag as the night began its assault of frigid air. Tommy's body radiated heat, he smelled of sweet body odor, and for not the first time she wondered why it had taken an asteroid plummeting into the Pacific Ocean for them to so much as speak to each other.

AUGUST 30TH

At first when she heard the sound, Angela assumed it was her stomach rumbling again. She lifted her head and stared at the sky. The moon shone down on her with its bluish glow, but she noticed clouds beginning to roll in once more. *Damn*, she thought. *Not more rain.* They couldn't afford to spend time indoors, not with the possibility of rescue. If the helicopters showed up again, they had to be out and ready.

The sound intensified, shaking her to the core, and she

rose to her feet, nudging Tommy awake in the process. He stirred and sat up.

"What's going on?"

"Helicopters, I think."

"At night?"

"I know. Weird."

A spotlight appeared in the distance. It was low, just barely skimming the surface of the water as it progressed from rooftop to rooftop. The water had risen dramatically of late, and now was only ten feet from overtaking them.

The helicopter hovered over a building. She couldn't tell exactly how far away they were in the dark, but it had to be close. She could hear muffled shouts and a bustle of activity. Soon more voices joined in. Their tone seemed joyous.

The Freemans yelled from their distant perch. "Is it another?" the father's voice asked, small as a mouse's.

"It is!" screamed Tommy.

Angela started jumping up and down, bellowing as loud as she could. "Over here! We're over here! Don't leave us!" Tommy joined in. Even together, their yells seemed to die inches in front of their faces.

The helicopter swerved around, its spinning blades beating a drumbeat of salvation. The spotlight pointed in their direction. It moved forward, approaching them, so close the wind from its rotors blew Angela's hair from her face.

It drifted slowly across the rippling water. A strange, violet glow appeared beneath it, like millions of fireflies below the surface. Angela's breath caught in her throat. From the ocean rose a giant hand that wrapped itself around the helicopter's frame. The blades cut through the water, and it seemed to scream. Then, quick as a blink, the helicopter was forced into the water nose-first. The rotors snapped. Angela felt a rush of air against her cheek. She threw her arm around Tommy and forced him to the ground. Shrapnel rained around them. Frightened screams echoed over the waves. Angela squeezed her eyes shut. She felt Tommy shudder and cry out.

This was it. She knew it.

Tears ran down her cheeks in torrents.

SEPTEMBER 1ST

Angela held Tommy close. A light drizzle fell, biting her flesh but not enough to make her move. She shivered in the cold breeze and held her breath. But for the waves, all was silent.

After a while she lifted her head. A gray haze dulled everything. She stood up and looked behind her. The Freemans were still huddled together on the roof of their building. None looked up at her, even when she called out to them. Dexter McCutchens was nowhere to be seen.

Water trickled over the retaining wall. She drifted to the side of the building, cringed, and looked down. The level had risen overnight, and the sea was choppy. Waves collided with the walls and flowed into the smashed windows on the level just below. She lifted her gaze, following the horizon line, taking in the new, watery world. Distant skyscrapers jutted from the sea as it slowly swallowed everything. And there were twinkling lights in the water now, the same sort of lights that came before the helicopter had been taken under the previous evening. She thought of those trapped inside the hulk of steel as it plunged beneath the ocean's surface. Were they devoured by whatever it was that had taken them? Did they drown? In either case it seemed a horrible way to go.

Thoughts of her family entered her mind, and Angela crumpled. She writhed on the concrete while acid rain washed over her. Had her mother and father succumbed to the same fate as those in the chopper? When the oceans rose, had their house in the Cape been among the first to go? Were they dead? Were they suffering?

Or had they found their own rooftop? Were they, like Angela, now hovering perilously close to the edge, surviving day-by-day, and waiting, just waiting, for the water to flood their sanctuary and bring them to the hungry mouths of whatever lay just beneath the surface?

She cried, long and hard. Her lungs and throat burned. She bellowed until she couldn't any longer and then lay there, shaking and whimpering, ready to give up.

A gentle hand touched her shoulder. Angela looked up through moist eyes. It was Tommy. Of course it was. He wore a half-smile on his face and gazed down at her with affection. She brought her hand up and touched his cheek. It was soft, despite lumps of irritation where the rain had hit it. He leaned in and planted his lips on hers. She went with it, running her tongue over his mouth, opening wide, taking in all the comfort he had to offer.

Tommy lifted her up and brought her to the tent. He placed her inside, sealed the flap, and gradually undressed her. His mouth found her again, moved from her lips to neck to breasts to belly, placing gentle pecks wherever the burning rain had left its mark.

They made love for the first time in the depressing, soggy haze of morning. There was no crying out in pleasure for either of them. No moans of satisfaction left their throats. There were only soft sighs in the darkness of the tent, moving in tune with the crashing waves, using each other's bodies for solace as if the gyrations could shake away the sorrow that had swallowed all hope.

SEPTEMBER 8TH

Overnight, the Freemans disappeared. Angela kept vigil on the side of the roof closest to their building, hoping they would appear from inside, hold up a sign, and tell them all was fine.

It never happened. They were simply...gone.

Angela's stomach rumbled. She doubled over in pain. Over the last few days, they'd run out of food and water. The last of the supplies Tommy had retrieved from the upper floors before they became submerged were gone. They'd thought they had plenty, surely enough to get them by until help arrived. Now all they had to sustain themselves were the pigeons that sometimes landed on the roof. But getting their hands on the birds proved a tedious task, at best. They'd caught only three over the last seven days, and had to tear them apart with bare hands and eat them raw. At first Angela thought she couldn't do it. Her savage hunger won out, however, and the second time she dove into the bloody meal like a starving lioness.

The worst, however, was the lack of water. They dared not drink the ocean water, even if they'd had the bravery to get close enough to obtain some. So they settled on gathering rainwater and drinking that. It was murky in their canteens and stung going down. Often they vomited after consuming it. But the body required water, and it was their only choice, so they dealt with it as best they could.

The ocean lights had begun to multiply, as well. They floated around the building like strings of Christmas lights, illuminating the evenings and casting a dull glow during the day. Angela decided that under different circumstances she might have found them pretty.

To pass the time, she and Tommy made love. Every day, three times or more. The act allowed them at least a few fleeting moments of normalcy, of comfort. They would lay in each other's arms afterward, shielded by their rapidly deteriorating tent, and talk about what they'd do when the world returned to normal. Not that either of them believed this would happen. Angela, for her part, was resigned to her eventual fate. Her only wish was to go on for one more day, despite the pain.

She was stubborn like that.

SEPTEMBER 12TH

"We need something to eat," said Tommy. "We need it now."

"I know," Angela replied, defeated. "But how are we gonna get some?"

The pigeons had ceased landing on the roof; like the Freemans, they seemed to have vanished. Even the seagulls, which she'd often noticed flocking around the tops of the taller skyscrapers as if they feared getting too close to the rising tides, were gone. It seemed the whole of the earth above the surface of the ocean had ceased to exist. For a moment Angela thought she and Tommy might be the last humans alive. She shuddered and forced that assumption from her mind.

"We can get some canned goods from the apartments," said Tommy. "There was still a bunch of stuff in there before they flooded. Even bottled water. It should still be fine."

"But we already talked about that. It...it's under water."

"I know. But heck, I can swim."

"But..."

Tommy's brow creased. His eyes looked tired. "There's no other choice, Ang. It's either that or starve."

They made their way down the stairs. At least the flooding hadn't reached that high yet. It wasn't until they reached the top floor that they saw the water. It glistened in the weak light coming from the stairwell but still appeared brown and dirty. Tommy plunged in. It came up to his waist. Angela followed. The water was cold. Goosebumps rose on her flesh.

They waded down the hallway until they reached apartment 14C. It was the old Beaulieu place, a nice older couple who'd fled, along with most of the city, when news of the impending flood spread. At the time, Angela had wanted to join them. It was Tommy, who lived in the apartment opposite hers, who came up with the idea to take refuge on the roof. *It takes hours to reach the Green Mountains*, he'd said. *And that's with no traffic. With everyone trying to reach higher ground, we'd be lucky to get there before the water gets us. Our best bet is to stay here and wait for help to come.*

They entered the apartment. Magazines and other detritus floated past them. Tommy led Angela to the kitchen. The countertops were just above the waterline, islands of white marble resting in a brown sea.

"I'm going under," Tommy said.

Angela swayed from side to side, her body growing numb in the cold water. "You need help?"

"I'll be fine."

Tommy dove beneath the surface. The water was so murky Angela couldn't see any part of him when he submerged. Air bubbles popped up in his place. Something brushed against her leg and she jumped, hoping beyond hope it was only Tommy as he rummaged through the lower cabinets.

A minute later he reemerged. He held a stack of canned vegetables. He placed them on the counter and winked at her.

"See, told you," he said. "And I think I felt a case of bottled water down there, too. I'll be right back."

With another deep breath, Tommy plunged back into the murk. Angela took a garbage bag from the shelves to her rear and loaded it with cans. Once more Tommy brushed her leg, only she didn't jump this time. She giggled a bit instead.

"You gotta be more careful!" she yelled at the rising bubbles. "One of these times you'll get a little too close to you-know-where, and then..."

Something caught her eye; flashes, like sparks, coming from the doorway. Slowly she turned her head. Through the opening appeared a clump of shimmering lights. It moved gradually, gracefully, like liquid within liquid, coming toward them. Angela backed up a step.

"Uh, Tommy?" She swallowed a lump, tried to call for him again, and couldn't. Fear choked her.

Tommy hadn't come up.

In a panic, she thrust her arms into the water. Her hands searched blindly for him, but came away with nothing. A quick glance told her the approaching tube of sludge and light was halfway across the kitchen. She searched harder. Her foot caught on something, and she fell forward. Her face splashed below the surface. Stinging salt water ran down her throat. She thrashed around, trying to regain her footing.

"Ang, what's wrong?"

Angela stopped her flailing and looked at the voice. Tommy stood before her, away from the counter, on the other side of the room. He held up a twelve-pack of Evian with his right hand, oblivious to the thing coming up behind him.

She opened her mouth to speak, but no words came out.

"Did I scare you? Sorry. I thought it'd be a good joke to swim around you. You know, surprise you a little. I guess it was a stupid idea."

The thing in the water started to encircle him. Tommy never saw it. He simply stared at Angela with a look of concern in his eyes. It wasn't until the thing's flashing, ethereal lights floated in front of him that he screamed.

A cylinder of flashing, brown water rose up and wrapped itself around his chest. One moment he was above water, the next he disappeared. Angela watched with eyes bulging, afraid to move. A swirl of air bubbles appeared where Tommy had stood.

Angela held her breath. All was quiet but for the sloshing of the water. She inched to the side, along the counter, heading for the door. Her elbow struck an open drawer. She winced but kept on going.

Tommy's head exploded from the water. Angela screamed. He lashed out with his arms like a drowning man. Strange veins of a substance that looked like seaweed clung to him, pulling him back under. He fought against it. The flesh on his neck singed. The brown water around him turned red. The veins then worked their way to his head. His eyes bulged, and he offered a gurgling, blood-filled scream before his cheeks caved in. A few more veins pulled off his lower jaw. It sank into the depths.

Angela dashed out of the kitchen fast as she could. The waist-deep water fought against her with nightmarish force. Tears streamed down her cheeks. In a few moments she was out of the apartment and back in the hallway. Still more clumps of shimmering light approached. She turned away and waded toward the stairs. She could feel their slimy fingers on her heels. The roof access door, still open, was only a few feet away.

Gasping and dripping water, she scurried up the stairs and never once looked back. When she got to the roof, she slammed the door shut and slid down it until her wet butt smacked the concrete.

She sat there and cried, with her head in her hands, for hours.

SEPTEMBER 15TH

It was night. Angela's stomach cramped. She lay on her back in the middle of the roof, staring up at a star-filled sky. She traced lines from one star to another, making pictures in her mind. Every one came out looking like Tommy.

Another pang wrenched her gut, and she moaned. She hadn't eaten in days. The polluted rainwater she drank tore up her insides. Her throat burned with every sip, and when she looked at her reflection in a puddle, she saw her cheeks were pallid and sunken. She looked like a corpse.

Growing bored and depressed, she rolled over and curled into a ball. She needed sleep, though it seemed sleep was all she did. She closed her eyes and hoped the next time she woke up it wouldn't be in the middle of a nightmare.

SEPTEMBER 22ND

Dry weather arrived, and when it did, the seas stopped rising. The water was only two feet from the top of the apartment building. Every so often, if there was a strong wind, waves would lash over the sides, covering the roof with brown, tainted water.

Not that Angela cared much. She had no food, no water, no hope. She lingered in the same spot for hours, staring at the cracks in the concrete below her. Her lips were dry and split, her body emaciated and dying.

Her eyes started playing tricks on her. As dehydration set in, she began to see ships in the distance; giant sea-faring vessels that towed nets filled with the remains of all the people she'd known. These ships always stayed just beyond the horizon, barely visible, never coming any closer. But to her mind's eye they were big as cities.

Maybe she should have been frightened, but she wasn't.

Another crack caught her attention, and she watched it.

SEPTEMBER 26TH

"King me."

Angela placed one checker on another and grinned. "Good job, Tommy," she said. "Why can't I ever beat you?"

"I'm just good," he replied.

She looked in his eyes. They were so kind and loving. She could gaze into them forever.

"So, what're you lovebirds doing?" asked another voice. Angela turned around. It was Rachid Freeman. He sat in a beach chair, bouncing his little daughter in his lap. He smiled, and his white teeth reflected the sunlight. Roberta approached, handed him a glass of iced tea, and squeezed his hand.

"It's so beautiful out today," she said.

"Sure is. Sun's shining, sand's not too hot, water's cool... could be the best day ever."

Angela grinned. She ran her hand through the sand. They were right. It *was* cool. She giggled, thinking herself silly for not noticing before.

"What's so funny?" asked Tommy.

"Oh, nothing," she replied. "I can just be ridiculous, you know?"

They reclined on a towel that hadn't been there a second ago and let the sun warm their flesh. "Can I ask you a question?" asked Tommy.

"Shoot."

"What do you want to do with your life?"

Angela cocked her head. "Do with my life? What kind of question is that?"

"Just curious."

"Oh, well, I don't know, really. Haven't thought about it much. I guess I'd like to have a good job and..." She bit her lip. "No, that's not right. I think, more than anything, I just want to be happy. I want to be in the moment and *live*. I've seen too many folks live like they're scared of life, and I don't want that to be me."

"So, how'll you pull that off?"

Angela flashed Tommy a mischievous grin. "Right now, by beating you into the water."

She stood up without hesitation and took off. Tommy was right behind her. She dashed across the beach as fast as her legs could carry her and then leapt from the rocks. Tucking her knees to her chest, she plunged beneath the water. As it washed over her she felt soothed by its coolness, especially on a day bright as this one. She wanted to bathe in that feeling forever.

She never came back up.

THE MEEK

Scott Nicholson

The ram hit Lucas low, twisting its head so that its curled horns knocked him off his feet. The varmint was good at this. It had killed before. But the dead eyes showed no joy of the hunt, only the black gleam of a hunger that ran wider than the Gibson.

Lucas winced as he sprawled on the ground, tasting desert dust and blood, his hunger forgotten. As the Merino tossed its head, the horns caught the strange sunlight and flashed like knives. Lucas had only a moment to react. He rolled to his left, reaching for his revolver.

The ram lunged forward, its lips parted and slobbering. The mouth closed around the ankle of Lucas's left boot. He kicked, and the spur raked across the ram's nose. Gray pus leaked from the torn nostrils, but the animal didn't even slow down in its feeding frenzy.

The massive head dipped again, going higher, looking for Lucas's flank. But Lucas wasn't ready to kark, not out here in the open with nothing but stone and scrub acacia to keep him company. Lucas filled his hand, ready to blow the ram back to Hell or wherever else it was these four-legged devils came from.

But he was slow, tired from four days in the saddle and weak from hunger. The tip of one horn knocked the gun from his hand, and he watched it spin silver in the sky before dropping to the sand ten feet away. Eagles circled overhead, waiting to clean what little bit of meat the animal would leave on his bones. He fell back, hoping his leather chaps would stop the teeth from gnawing into his leg.

Just when he was ready to shut his eyes against the coming horror, sharp thunder ripped the sky open.

At first he thought it was Gabriel's trumpet, harking and heralding and all that. Then Lucas was covered in the explosion of brain, bits of skull, and goo as the ram's head disappeared. The animal's back legs folded, and then it collapsed slowly upon itself. It fell on its side and twitched once, then lay still, thick fluid dribbling from the stump of its neck.

Gun smoke filled the air, and the next breath was the sweetest Lucas had ever taken. He sat up and brushed the corrupted mutton from his face, then checked to make sure the animal's teeth hadn't broken his skin. The chaps were intact, with a few new scrapes in the leather.

"'bout got you," came a raspy voice. Lucas cupped his hand over his eyes and squinted as a shadow fell over him. The man was bow-legged, his rifle angled with the stock against his hip, the white avalanche beard descending from a Grampian mountain range of a face.

"Thank you, mate," Lucas said, wiping his mouth. "And thank the Lord for His mercy."

The old man kicked at the carcass, and it didn't move. He spat a generous rope of tobacco juice onto the oozing neck wound. Flies had already gathered on the corpse. Lucas hoped that flies didn't turn into flesh-eating critters, too. Having dead-and-back-again sheep coming after you was plenty bad enough.

"A stray. Third one today," the old man said, working the Remington's action so that the spent shell kicked free. He stooped to read the brand on the ram's hip. "Come from

Kulgera. They never could keep 'em rounded up down those parts."

Lucas struggled to his feet, sore from the sheep-wrestling. He found his hat and secured it on his head, then returned his revolver to its holster. "If you hadn't come along when you did—"

The man cut in, his eyes bright with held laughter. "Hell, son, I been watching you for five minutes. Wasn't sure which of you was going to walk away. I'd have put two-to-one on the Merino, but nobody much left around to take the bet."

Lucas thought about punching the stranger in the face, but Lucas was afraid his hand would shatter against that stone-slick surface. The man must have seen the anger in Lucas's eyes, because the laugh busted free of the thin lips, rolling across the plateau like the scream of a dying wombat.

"Never you mind," the man said, slapping the barrel of his Remington. "I'd sooner sleep with a brown snake than watch a man get ate up."

He held his hand out. It was wrapped in a glove the color of a chalky mesa, stained a rusty red. Lucas took it and shook quickly, feeling a strength in the grip that didn't match the man's stringy muscles.

"Name's Camp," he said.

"Lucas," Lucas said. "Is 'Camp' short for something?"

"Not that I know of. Just Camp, is all."

"You're not Aussie."

"Hell, no. Come from Texas, U.S. of A. Had to leave 'cause the damned place was pert near run over by Mexicans and Injuns. You know how it is, when the furriners come in and take over, don't you?"

Lucas nodded and said, "Things are crook in Musclebrook, no doubt." He walked toward his horse twenty yards away, to where it had fallen in a shallow gulley. Camp followed, solemn now. Nobody laughed at the loss of a good horse.

The horse whinnied softly, froth bubbling from its nose. A hank of flesh had been ripped from its side. The saddle strap had broken, tossing Lucas's canteen and lasso into a patch of saltbrush. The horse's tail whisked at the air, swatting invisible flies.

"Never thought I'd see the day a sheep could outrun a horse," Camp said.

"Never thought I'd see a lot of things," Lucas answered.

Camp spat again, and a strand of the brown juice clung to his beard. He was the first person Lucas had ever met who chewed tobacco. "Want to borrow my Remington?" he asked, holding out the rifle.

"Mate's got to do it his own way."

"Reckon so," Camp said, then turned so as not to see the tears in Lucas's eyes.

Lucas drew the revolver and put two bullets in the horse's head. Vickie, he'd called her. Had her for six years, had roped and broken her himself. Now she was nothing but eagle food. But at least she wouldn't rise up tonight, bucking and kicking and hungry for a long mouthful of the hand that had once fed her.

"Where you headed?" Camp asked when they'd reached the top of the gulley.

Lucas scanned the expanse of plateau ahead of them. Finally he shrugged. "I was mostly headed away from something, not toward something."

"Sheep's everywhere now, is the word. Perth, Adelaide, Melbourne, all your big transport cities. They roam the streets scrounging for ever scrap of human cud they can find."

"Even back Queensland?"

"Queensland got it bad. 'course, them damned banana

benders deserve everything they get, and then some." Camp took a plug of tobacco from his shirt pocket that looked like a dry dingo turd. He bit into it with his four best teeth, then worked it until he could spit again. He held out the plug to Lucas.

"No. You're a gent, though." Lucas was thirsty. He took a swig from his canteen, thought about offering a drink to Camp, then shuddered at the thought of the man's backwash polluting the water.

"I'm headed for Wadanetta Pass. Hear word there's a bunch holed up there."

"I didn't know some were trying to fight," Lucas said. "I figured it was every bloke for himself."

He hadn't seen another person for three days, at least not one that was alive. He'd passed a lump of slimy dress this morning, a bonnet on the ground beside it. Might have been one of them pub girls, or some schoolmarm fallen from a wagon. The sight had about made him launch a liquid laugh.

"You hungry?" Camp asked.

"Nobody not? What the blooming hell is there to eat out here except weeds and poisoned meat? It was a fair go I'd have ended up eating my horse, and I liked my horse."

"Wadanetta is thataway," Camp said, pointing into the shimmering layers of heat that hung in the west. "Might reach it before night."

"Damn well better. I don't want to be out here in the dark with that bunch playing sillybuggers."

"Amen to that." Camp led the way, moving as if he had a gun trained on his back. It was all Lucas could do to keep up.

They walked in silence for about half an hour. Lucas's feet were burning in his boots. He was about convinced that Hell lay only a few feet beneath the plains and that the devil was working up to the biggest jimbuck roundup of all time. First killer sheep, then a sun that glowed like a bloody eye.

"Suppose it's like this all about?" Lucas asked.

"You mean, out Kimberly and all that?"

"New Zealand. Guinea."

"Don't see why not. Sheep are sheep all over the world."

"Even over in England?"

"Bloody hope so."

"Beaut," said Lucas. "That bugger, God, ought to be half sporting, you'd think."

"Hell, them Merino probably would stoop to eating Aborigines. I heared of a country run all by darkies, hardly a white man there. These darkies, they worship cows. I mean, treat them like Jesus Christ come again."

Lucas almost smiled at that one. "Cows likely went over with the sheep. Bet the darkies changed their tune a little by now."

"Them what's left," Camp said, punctuating the sentence with tobacco spit.

They walked on as the sun sank lower and the landscape became a little rougher. A few hills rolled in the distance, dotted with scrub. They came to a creek, and Lucas pointed out the hoofprints in the muddy banks.

They stopped for a drink and to rest a few minutes, then continued. The day was an hour from dark when they reached the base of a steep mesa. The cliffs were eroded from centuries of wind and weather. A small group of wooden humpies huddled in the shadow of the mesa.

"Wadanetta, dead ahead," Camp said. They broke into a jog. When they were a hundred yards away from the town, they shouted. Their voices echoed off the stone slopes. Nobody came from the gray buildings to greet them.

"Anybody here?" Lucas yelled as they reached a two-story building that looked like a knock shop. Camp pushed open the door. The parlor was empty, a table knocked over, playing cards spread across the floor. A piano sat in one corner, with a cracked mug on top.

They went inside, and Lucas yelled again. The only answer was the creaking of wood as a sunset wind arose. "Thought you said blokes was here," Lucas said.

"Said I heared it. Hearing and knowing is different things."

Camp walked around the bar and knocked on one of the wooden kegs that lined the shelf. "They left some grog."

He grabbed a mug and drew it full. In the fading light, the lager looked like piss, flat and cloudy. Camp wrinkled his nose and took a drink without bothering to remove his chaw. He swished the ale around and swallowed.

"Any good?" Lucas asked, eyeing the stairs, expecting some grazed-over jackaroo to come stumbling down with his pants around his ankles.

"Nope," said Camp, but he quickly drained the rest of his glass and refilled it.

Lucas pulled a stool out from the bar and sat down. He thought about trying the ale, but decided against it. Night was nearly here, and he didn't want to be slowed down by drunkenness. "What do we do for a bite?"

"Well, we can't eat no mutton, that's for damned sure."

"I've been eating kangaroo. Hasn't karked me yet, but I used up the last of it a couple of days ago. Thought about killing a rabbit, but it's hard to bang one with a pistol."

"How do you know rabbits don't got it, same as the sheep?"

"Rabbits haven't been eating people."

"Least as far as you know."

Lucas had to nod in agreement.

Camp gulped down another mugful and wiped his mouth on his sleeve. "Nearly time."

Lucas nodded again. "Saw a general store up the street. Might have some rifles and ammo."

Camp pulled another ale, the yeasty stench filling the room. Or maybe it was Camp himself that stank. "You go ahead. I'm aiming to knock back one or two more, to get my nerve up."

Lucas got off the stool and went outside, pausing on the porch to make sure no sheep had strayed from the herd. The sun was almost gone now, the west streaked with purple and pink rags. It had been three weeks since Lucas had last watched a sunset without dread crawling through his bones. Three weeks since a sheep was just a sheep. Things go full-on berko real fast.

He went up the street, his hand on the butt of his revolver. Something rustled in an alley to his left. He spun and drew, his hand trembling. A crumpled hat blew out into the street. He sagged in relief.

He shook like a blue-assed fly in a windstorm. He pulled the brim of his hat low over his eyes, glad no one was around to see him like this. Word got around fast when a fellow broke down.

A small rise of land to the left was bathed in the dying sunlight. A few wooden crosses still stood askew, but the picket fence marking off the cemetery had been trampled into ruin. Wadanetta's boneyard had been plowed up by gut-hungry sheep. Lucas pictured a whole herd of them, pawing and snorting to bust into those pine boxes and get at the goods inside.

He hurried to the general store. It was just as desolate as the knock shop had been. Cobwebs hung on the shelves, but he found a few blankets and a box of bullets for the revolver. All the rifles were gone. Some money was left in the register. Lucas didn't take it.

Camp staggered into the store, his Remington over his

shoulder. "Could have told you they'd be no rifles," he said, his words slurred. "I took the last one."

"Bloody hell? You been here before?"

"We'd best get over to the jail. Sheep smell us, they'll be going crazy. They might be able to climb stairs, I don't know. But they sure as hell can't bust through steel bars."

They went into the street again, Camp leading the way. A soft bleating swept in from across the plateau. It was followed by another, then more of the man-eating sheep raised their voices.

"Ever wonder who's riding herd on them things?" Camp asked, not slowing.

Lucas looked behind them and saw a dust cloud roiling on the horizon. Appeared to be several hundred of them. The drum of hoofbeats filled the air. He hoped the jail was well built.

"I mean, you figure it's the devil or something?" Camp said, belching. "A sister from Lady of the Faith Church told me them which don't repent would have the devil to pay someday. Figure maybe someday's finally here?"

"I don't deadcert know," Lucas said, his voice thin from fright.

Darkness was settling like molasses, clogging Lucas's lungs and tightening his throat. He saw the jail and almost wept in relief. It was brick, squat, and solid, with iron bars across the windows.

Camp pulled a key from his pocket and opened the thick wooden door. A pungent odor struck Lucas like a fist. The stink reminded him of something, but the hoofbeats were so much louder now that they filled his senses, bounced around in his skull, drove every thought from his brain but the thought of sanctuary.

He stumbled into the dark room, and Camp closed the door behind them. Camp dropped a crossbar into place, then shook it in its hasps. "Safe as milk," he said. "Let's see them woolly-eyed buggers bust into here."

Lucas bumped into a table. He ran his hands over its surface. Something fell to the floor, and glass shattered. Flies buzzed around his head.

"Damn," Camp said. "You busted my lamp."

The stench was stronger, so thick that Lucas could barely breathe. The herd was closer now, stampeding into Wadanetta, a hundred haunted *bahs* bleating from bottomless mouths.

Camp's voice came from somewhere near the wall. "I like to watch them come in," he said. "They's something lovely about it. 'specially when the moon's up, and all them eyes are sparkling."

Lucas put his hands over his ears, squeezing tight to drive out the noises of the stampede. He thought of all the people who had filled those bellies, who had been stomped and ground into haggis, who had served as leg of lamb for this devil's herd. The first of the horns rattled off the brick. The building shook, but Camp laughed.

"They can't get us in here," the old man shouted over the din. "You'd figure the dumb bastards would quit trying. But night after night they come back. Guess I ought to quit encouraging them."

A match flared. Camp's face showed in the orange circle of light. He sat beside the window, grinning, his rotted teeth like mossy tombstones. He pointed the Remington at Lucas's heart.

Lucas forgot about the sheep. He'd had guns pointed at him a time or two before. But never like this, with his guard so far down. He was in no shape for a quick draw.

"Don't try it," Camp said. "You might be fast, maybe not, but you're not likely faster than a bullet."

Horn and snout hammered against the window bars.

Camp put the bobbing matchlight to the end of a candle. The room grew a little brighter, and Lucas saw what stank so badly.

Naked bodies, three of them, hanging upside down from chains inside one of the cells. One of them might have been a woman, judging from the swells in the red rags of flesh, but Lucas couldn't be sure. His heartbeat matched the rumble of the herd outside.

"Remember out there, when I rescued you, and I said I don't like to see a man get ate up?" Camp said, his voice as low and sinister as that of the sheep. "Don't like to let good meat go to waste, seeing as how it's getting so scarce and all. This free-range hunting is hell on an old man like me."

Camp sat on a chair, the rifle barrel steady. Lucas held his hands apart. He could see the tabletop, scarred and pitted, a dark and thick liquid on it. A nun's habit was folded over the back of a chair.

"Our Sister of the Lady of the Faith," Camp said, picking at his teeth with a thumbnail. "Mighty good eating. Figure it's the pureness of the flesh what makes it so sweet."

Lucas wouldn't have minded going down from a bullet. In fact, he'd always suspected that's the way he'd meet the Lord. Beat getting eaten by a Merino any day. But to know that this greasy bugger would be carving him into dinner portions was more than he could stomach.

"Hell, it's the way of things," Camp said, tilting back in his chair. "People eat sheep, then sheep eat people. What's so wrong about people eating people?"

Something slammed against the door, and two horn tips poked through the wood beneath the crossbar. Camp turned to look, and Lucas knew it was time. He rolled to his left, filling his hand with his oldest friend the revolver, and squeezed off three rounds without thinking. Camp gave a gasp of pain, and the Remington clattered to the floor.

Lucas lifted himself up and blew the smoke from the revolver's barrel. Camp slumped in the chair, holes in his chest. The scent of fresh blood aroused the herd, and heads butted frantically against the brick walls. Camp's eyes flickered, the light in them dying like the last stars of morning.

Lucas wondered how long the herd would mill around. Daylight usually made them get scarce, but one or two of the orneriest would probably hang around. Maybe they'd get rewarded for their trouble if they just happened to find some fresh meat out on the porch. One thing for sure, Camp would be nothing but gristle and rawhide. Hardly worth fooling with.

Lucas sat at the table. He'd heard that other people had turned to it, but the thought had sickened him. Until he'd run out of kangaroo. Hardly seemed unreasonable anymore, even for a man who followed the Lord. Camp's logic of the food chain fit right in with these balls-up times. And Lucas's stomach was squealing with all the intensity of a fresh-branded sheep.

Camp had been a fine butcher. The meat was thin and tender. Lucas stuck Camp's butcher knife into a slice and held it under his nose, checking its scent. Hell, not much different from mutton, when you got right down to it. His belly ached from need, and he wondered if that's how the sheep felt.

He chewed thoughtfully. The taste wasn't worth savoring, but it wasn't so terrible that he spat it out. He speared a second piece and held it up to the candlelight.

"You know, Sister," he addressed the meat. "Maybe you were right. Someday might just be here after all."

Maybe the Good Book was right, too, that the meek were busy inheriting the earth at this very moment. Lucas figured it would be humble and proper to offer up a word of prayerful thanks. He bowed his head in silence, then continued with the meal that the Holy Father had provided.

Outside, in the dark ghost town of Wadanetta, the chorus of sheep voiced its eternal hunger.

SOURDOUGH

RUTH FRANCISCO

As Gillian Stabler stood among the tomato cages in her garden, picking green worms off the vines and squishing them beneath her clog, she thought she detected a change in the atmosphere. It felt like a warm breath, or that peculiar heat you feel when someone is staring at you from a distance.

She straightened her back, her eyes sweeping over her neat rows of vegetables. The early morning sun beamed through the chard and eggplants, making their furcated leaves look like veins. Was that a pulse she felt under her feet? A heartbeat?

She scanned the yard and looked deep into the swamp behind the house. She saw no one. Nothing appeared out of place.

Gillian was seldom subject to bursts of panic. She prided herself on being pragmatic and levelheaded. She believed that a well-planned, orderly life brought domestic happiness and that any conflict could be resolved if people simply sat down and discussed their differences sensibly.

Gillian and her husband, Tom, lived in a small affluent suburb outside of San Francisco. Tom was a research scientist at UC Berkeley—something to do with organic compounds—and spent most of his time hunched over a computer. Gillian taught high school English and took the summers off. As a couple, they were well suited. They argued over the daily paper to their mutual enjoyment, often collaborating on long-winded letters to the editor. Tom was faithful (except for that one incident with a French exchange student), and still surprised Gillian with flowers and gifts. Nearly every week, he kidnapped her (as she called it), whisking her off to a special restaurant or to the theater. Once even to Hawaii.

A nearly perfect life for a nearly perfect couple.

But this morning at the breakfast table, Gillian had read in the paper that the hole in the ozone over Antarctica had expanded to the size of North America. Gillian, like any careful reader of *The New York Times*, was concerned about the melting snows of Kilimanjaro, the disappearing glaciers in the Bolivian Andes, the disintegrating Arctic ice shelf, the soggy permafrost, and the vanishing rain forests, but this hole in the ozone made her uneasy to the point of distress. Then Tom—her husband of fifteen years, a man whom she thought she knew—had the gall to say, "Media hysteria, my dear; nothing to worry about. The world is always changing. There's global warming, global cooling, global expanding, global shrinking. It's perfectly normal, sweetheart."

Gillian was stunned. She and Tom *never* disagreed about such things. She looked at him disdainfully, not recognizing this stranger in her kitchen, this confident middle-aged man with thinning hair, in a crisp starched shirt and khakis, who chomped noisily on his bagel, eyes glued to the sports section. Without replying, she took her coffee into the garden.

As Gillian stepped between the rows of carrots and radishes, she pictured the earth as a leaking balloon that might suddenly zip off its orbit, deflating as it shot across the Milky Way. She looked into the sky, half expecting to see clouds swirling into a dark blue hole, like water down a drain. What if something dropped into the hole from outside, like asteroids, or aliens? When she leaned over the lettuce, she thought she detected a slight lifting in the air, as if she and everything around her were being sucked up.

Earthquakes, tsunamis—freakish weather patterns seemed ever more frequent. The tectonic plates at the bottom of the Indian Ocean had slid beneath one another. The earth was smaller, spinning faster. There were holes in the sky. The planet had shifted on its axis by an inch! The world was out of balance. How could Tom possibly say that nothing was wrong?

No, no, she mustn't let herself get all worked up about something she couldn't change. After taking three deep breaths, Gillian picked up the colander she had brought from the kitchen and set about gathering salad greens before the wilting heat of the day. The rhythm of the work calmed her some, yet her uneasiness lingered.

A little before noon, Gillian's neighbor, Mrs. Gunther, dropped by. Mrs. Gunther was an attractive woman in her sixties, a piano teacher who looked after her paraplegic husband, a socialist poet of some renown. She brought Gillian a white ceramic bowl of sourdough starter. *Friendship bread*, she called it, because the tasty starter was shared between friends. It made excellent sourdough pancakes, Mrs. Gunther said, with just the right amount of tang. She gave Gillian several recipes, but, she warned, every seven days the starter had to be fed and then used.

"You save a little bit for next time," she explained.

"What happens if you don't use it after seven days?" asked Gillian.

Mrs. Gunther didn't know. She had always baked up something before then.

Gillian was pleased with this new domestic project. She first used the starter to make sourdough bread, then tried pancakes, muffins, cakes, and breakfast rolls. Tom loved everything, particularly the sourdough pancakes.

Several weeks later, Gillian jolted awake in the middle of the night, her heart pounding loudly. She sat up in bed, listening. Tom, asleep beside her, hummed quietly as he exhaled. A cat yowled several houses away. She swung her legs off the bed, carefully, so as not to disturb Tom, slipped on her slippers, and went downstairs to the kitchen.

Moonlight poured through the windows, polishing the fixtures and countertops.

So beautiful, she thought. *So orderly and clean.*

Her eyes followed the contours of the appliances, all in their assigned places. She delighted in the symmetrical shapes, which in the dramatic light created a Mondrian composition.

But something was out of place. The bowl of sourdough starter was in the middle of the counter. She had been keeping it out of the way in the corner under the hanging pot of Boston ivy. But there it was, a circle in a perfect square of light, basking like a moon flower. Why would Tom move it there? He almost never came into the kitchen.

Then she remembered that tomorrow was the seventh day since the last time she had used it. Perhaps Tom, now fond of the sourdough flavor, had moved the bowl there to remind her. But Tom could never keep track of temporal cycles, and was always surprised by monthly bills, her periods, dentist check-ups, birthdays, and anniversaries. "Is it that time again?" he would say astonished. It seemed unlike him to remember about the sourdough.

Gillian lifted the plastic that covered the bowl, feeling a little apprehensive, as if she were violating its privacy. The dough was nearing the rim; its dimpled top looked indecent. Spurred on by a delicious surge of malevolence, she stuck her finger in the middle and watched the dough shrivel, leaving long strings of dough attached to the sides of the bowl.

They look like stretch marks, she thought with revulsion.

In a panic, she grabbed a rubber spatula and scraped down the sides of the bowl until the dough was a neat little mound in the center. She rinsed off the spatula with hot water and put it in the dish rack. Then she covered the bowl with clear plastic and shoved it back into the corner under the ivy.

She was breathing rapidly, and there was a metallic taste in her mouth, almost like blood. She sat at her cozy pine table and chuckled nervously. Imagine, getting so upset over a bowl of bread dough! She realized she was bored of the seven-day routine, bored of baking, bored of having her life dictated by a yeasty mixture of flour and water. Tomorrow, she would make one last recipe and use all of the dough.

With this decided, Gillian felt at peace. She shuffled back to bed with a pleasant sense of expectation.

The next morning, Tom woke her to a breakfast tray with coffee, orange juice, strawberries, and a croissant. He was in a playful mood. It was their anniversary, he said, and he was going to take her on an adventure.

Of course it wasn't their anniversary, but Gillian, delighted, threw on a denim skirt and a sweater and let herself be led by the hand to the garage.

They drove north up the California coast and stopped at a state park where they rode horses on the beach to a small seafood restaurant. They drank beer, ate clams, fed each other morsels of bread drenched in marinara sauce, then napped in the dunes. Later they drove back in the dark feeling relaxed, completely satisfied with their life together.

It was only after Gillian had slipped on a lacy peacock-blue chemise (a present from Tom) that she remembered the sourdough—she had forgotten to use it.

Oh well. A day or two couldn't make that much difference. At worst, the starter would be spoiled and she'd have a good excuse for throwing it out. She was still slightly tipsy from the afternoon's beer, and Tom was nibbling on her toes, so she decided to deal with it in the morning.

A little after midnight, she awoke feeling anxious. She smelled a cloying perfume in the damp night air—something like hops, but sweet and light and sexy. Like a night flower blossoming in the swamp. She went downstairs to the kitchen for a glass of water. The odor was more pungent; it tickled her nostrils. As she opened the kitchen door, she glanced at the bowl of sourdough. She sighed with relief to see it in its corner.

Still tense, she sat down with her favorite Italian cookbook—reading recipes always calmed her. Perhaps she would make Tom a special dinner tomorrow and announce it was his birthday.

Soon she was lost in a recipe: quail with Gorgonzola and prosciutto. She heard something that sounded like a burp and looked around. The windows were open. Perhaps there was a frog in the garden. She tried not to look at the bowl, but she couldn't help herself. The plastic stretched several inches above the rim. She decided to ignore it and turned a page in her cookbook to a recipe for rabbit in caper sauce.

Plop!

She *knew* what that was. She reached for the rubber spatula. A white mound of dough lay glistening on the Formica. As she scooped it up, another glob of dough plopped onto her hand. For a second, she almost imagined she could feel it moving, wriggling across her fingers. She cried out, repulsed. She rushed to the sink, swishing hot water over her hands until all the white clots disappeared down the drain.

Plop! Plop!

She turned and saw the dough spilling over the sides of the bowl. She ripped off the plastic and beat the dough with the spatula. It deflated into a tiny ball. She wiped up all the dough on the counter, then sprayed the surface with Windex for good measure. She considered dumping the rest down the sink, but hesitated—it might clog the pipes. She knew she was overreacting, but she didn't care. The idea of eating anything else cooked with the dough made her queasy.

What then? Toss it out on the compost?

No, she'd wrap it up in a trash bag and bring it to the curb for the garbage collectors.

But not now. Weariness overtook her, and she stumbled off to bed. She'd deal with it in the morning.

Early the next day, the telephone rang. It was Mrs. Gunther. Her voice was unusually agitated. Her eldest son, Richard, and his wife had visited her last night hoping she could help them sort out a disagreement. They'd talked for hours, hashing things out until Mrs. Gunther thought she'd finally calmed them down. But after she went to bed, the quarreling resumed. Her daughter-in-law somehow managed to fall through the sliding glass door in the living room and was now in the hospital. Mrs. Gunther hated to ask Gillian to get involved, but she had to take her husband to the doctor and wouldn't be able to get to the hospital until later that afternoon. Could Gillian go and hold Richard's hand until she got there? She was very worried about his state of mind.

Gillian almost asked why she didn't reschedule her husband's appointment but realized Mrs. Gunther wouldn't be calling if that had been an option.

She told her it was no problem, that she was happy to help. She turned off the coffee pot, threw on jeans and a tweed blazer, and stuffed an apple and the latest issue of *The New Yorker* into her purse. As she turned to close the kitchen door, her eyes fell on the bowl of sourdough.

I'll get rid of it when I get back, she thought and locked the door.

Richard was contrite, his large athletic body caved in over his knees. He had been weeping. It turned out that his wife didn't exactly *fall* through the sliding glass door. He had only meant to keep her from scratching him, he said. When the doctor came out of the operating room and reported that his wife would be all right, Richard began to blubber again. Gillian held his hand and told him that all marriages had their rough times, and that working through their differences would bring them closer together. It surprised Gillian to realize that she didn't believe a word she said. Richard, however, seemed comforted.

Mrs. Gunther didn't show up at the hospital until eight in the evening. When Gillian got home, it was close to nine. She was exhausted. Tom teased her about being Florence Nightingale. He ordered her to bed, brought her a hot toddy, and read to her from a slim volume of Pablo Neruda love poems. Soon she fell asleep.

Hours later, Gillian woke to a buzzing sound. It was dark, and the moon was full. The smell of hops made the air seem thick and hard to breathe. She scrambled downstairs. The kitchen door opened with resistance. The buzzing was louder and pulsing. As she walked in, something cold and wet grabbed her ankle. She opened her lips to scream; a glob of dough fell from the ceiling and plugged her mouth. Frantic, she spit it out and wiped it off her face, but her hand stuck. She twisted around in horror.

The dough was a foot deep, climbing over the stove, the walls, and the refrigerator. She tried to run, but the dough rooted her down. She glanced desperately at the window—the screen was black with hornets attracted by the sweet yeasty smell. The buzzing was unbearable. Prying her hand from her face, she picked up the broom and beat down the dough. But this time, it didn't shrivel up.

If only she could get to the stove, she could cook the dough and kill it. She pulled up one knee with both hands and yanked her foot free. Stepping toward the stove, she reached for the knobs for the front burners. She put all of her weight on her front leg and lunged. Her foot slipped and she fell, her arms sinking into the dough. She couldn't even scream.

Slowly, the dough bubbled over her and buried her.

The next morning, Tom sprang out of bed feeling young and energetic. He looked at the empty half of the bed and figured Gillian was out jogging. He was so lucky, he thought, to have a wife who kept in such good shape. He felt proud and grateful. Why not make breakfast and have it ready for her when she got back? He pulled on his sweatpants and went down to the kitchen.

He noticed the bowl of sourdough in the corner. Hadn't Gillian said that it needed using? What a great idea! He'd make sourdough pancakes. He broke an egg into the bowl, added milk and baking powder, melted butter on the griddle, and poured the first spoonful of batter.

As he stacked the golden griddlecakes on a platter, he glanced outside. The screen was covered with dozens of dead hornets. How strange. He'd ask Gillian to clean it when she had a chance. Quite morbid really.

He took the pancakes to the picnic table outside and served himself two, drenching them in maple syrup. How delicious!

Unable to stop himself, he ate another, and then another, until he'd consumed them all. Every last one of them.

RICKMAN'S PLASMA

WILLIAM MEIKLE

He would call it "Soundscapes of the City," and it would make him his fortune, of that Rickman was certain.

How could it fail?

All it had taken was a reconfigured dream machine. Courtesy of Dreamsoft Productions, a particularly skilled burglar, and the latest software from MYTH OS, Rickman's visions of bringing his music to the world were now that much closer to reality.

For the past forty nights he'd sampled and tweaked, taking the raw sounds that streamed into his loft apartment from the city outside. He merged them with his dream compositions and formed them into a holographic construct of sound and light and ionized gas, an ever-moving plasma bubble that hung like a giant amoeba in the center of his room.

As they swam, his creations sang, orchestrated overtures to the dark beauty of the night.

It had been a long hard journey to this point. During those first few days everything was sharp and jagged, harsh mechanical discordances that, while they had a certain musical quality, were not what he needed...not if he was going to take the world by storm. The plasma had roiled and torn, refusing to take a permanent shape, and Rickman despaired of what the city was telling him. Everything was ugly, mean-spirited. The music of the city spoke only of despair and apathy, and his dreams didn't make a dent when he overlaid them.

Then he had his epiphany.

Aptly, it came to him in a dream.

It starts with thin whistling, like a simple peasant's flute played at a far distance. At first all is black. The flute stops, and the first star flares in the darkness. And with it comes the first chord, a deep A-minor that sets the darkness spinning. The blackness resolves itself into spinning masses of gas that coalesce and thicken into great clouds of matter reaching critical mass and exploding into a symphony. Stars wheel overhead in a great dance, the music of the spheres cavorting in his head.

Rickman jumped from his bed and pointed his antenna toward the sky.

Almost immediately he got results.

The plasma formed a sphere, a ball of silver held in the holographic array. At first it just hung there in space, giving out a deep bass hum that rattled his teeth and set all the glassware in the apartment ringing.

Things changed quickly when he overlaid his dreams.

Shapes formed in the plasma, concretions that slid and slithered, rainbow light shimmering over their surface like oil on water. They sang as they swam, and Rickman soon found that by moving the antenna he was able to get the plasma to merge or to multiply, each collision or split giving off a new chord, the plasma taking on solid form.

But it still wasn't right.

The really good stuff only really started to happen this very night. He played back his previous recordings while keeping the antenna pointed skyward.

The plasma roiled.

The sounds became louder, more insistent, especially when he pointed at a certain patch of sky.

Soon he had a repeating beat going, with a modulated chorus above it that rose in intensity, and rose again as the plasma started to pulse.

He set his recorders going and started experimenting, feeding the recordings back to the plasma through his one-thousand-watt speakers, merging the sounds with the compositions from his dreams.

Within the hour the globe of plasma was responding to his dream overlays. When he played the recordings back at full volume the plasma swelled. The music grew, the chords overlapping one another in an orchestrated dance.

Rickman was so excited that he didn't notice the walls of his apartment beat in time to the music.

Nor did he spot that when he turned his back, the plasma ball grew, stretching like an inflating balloon. Cobalt blue colors flashed and it *surged.*

Rickman was its first victim.

The cops arrived ten minutes later in response to a neighbor's complaints about the noise.

When they burst in the door a plasma ball of rainbow colors rose to dance in the air in front of them, a swirling aura of gold and purple and black.

The sound started.

It was low at first, almost inaudible, but it rose to a crescendo until their ears were buffeted with raucous, mocking piping; a cacophony of high fluting that crashed discordantly over them.

Then the smell hit them, the fetid, unmistakable odor of death that caught at the back of the throat and threatened to send their guts into spasm.

The cops ran.

They didn't look back, and all the time the crazed fluting danced in the air around them. They called for help; but each shout only brought a fresh *surge* in the plasma. The air above the plasma crackled with electricity, blue static running over the formless mass.

It dragged itself across the floor, leaving a grey glistening streak of slime behind.

Within the protoplasm things moved, detached bones flowing, scraps of clothing fused with unidentifiable pieces of flesh. The surface boiled in numerous small lesions that bubbled and split like pieces of over-ripe fruit.

But worst of all was the source of the fluting. A huge, red, meaty maw pulsed wetly in time with the cacophony.

The younger cop made it to the elevator and slammed the button. He screamed, frustrated, as the doors slowly opened. He let them part just enough to slip inside then turned to look for his partner.

She was less than two yards from him, arms outstretched, pleading. He began to move toward her, but she stopped and jerked backward like a marionette. Her mouth opened wide into a scream, and she fell forward, her right hand hitting the *down* button even as he stretched out vainly.

The door began to close and, no matter how much he strained at it, he was unable to stop it from shutting completely. He could do nothing but watch the events in the hallway beyond through the elevator's small window.

The plasma had caught her by the ankle. Oily colors flowed across her body, the protoplasm gripping her tight.

She struggled hard to no avail.

Their eyes met, just once. Her mouth opened as if she was trying to speak, and that was when the swirling blob engulfed her head and the noises from her throat ceased to sound human.

The protoplasm *surged* again, and suddenly the window of the cab was coated with slime.

The cop gagged and fought hard to keep down the bile as a human foot, still trailing bloody threads behind it, floated across his view.

The cop spent the next fifteen minutes persuading his superiors that there was a problem in the tower block. In that time the plasma ate the little old lady in number 621 who played her radio too loud, the three kids jamming on electric guitars in 437 and the family in 223 who had been watching the latest Disney animation on their 60-inch TV.

By the time the cop's backup team arrived it had already filled the whole of the ground floor public area. The cop made sure he was first back through the door, but what met him made him step back immediately.

A shimmering rainbow blob nearly four feet thick covered the floor. There were things embedded in it—blood and hair and bones and eyes, fused and running in to one another as if assembled by a demented sculptor. And in the middle of the floor something rose up out of the mass, a forearm stripped to the bone, skeletal fingers reaching for the roof. On each fingertip a grey, opaque eyeball stared blindly out at him.

That wasn't the worst thing though. The worst thing was the way the bones of the wrist cracked and groaned as the hand turned, the fingers flexing and bending as all five eyes rolled and stared straight at him. The mocking cacophony of high fluting crashed discordantly over him.

He raised his gun and fired.

The noise echoed loudly in the hallway.

The plasma surged again, enfolding the cop until he fell

into it, like a drowning man going down for the last time. The plasma rolled forward, forcing its way out onto the sidewalk beyond.

The backup team saw what happened to the cop. They started in with their own weapons.

The air filled with the noise of gunfire.

The plasma *surged* and took them.

Sirens blared as the squad cars of more backup teams arrived in the street.

The plasma *surged* and took them too.

The mayor got involved ten minutes later. Assembled in his room were the chief of police, the mayor's press officer and the chief of the fire service.

"So what is it doing now?" the mayor asked.

"Still growing," the chief of police answered. "And still feeding." The policeman was white as a sheet and trembling.

"How many casualties?" the mayor whispered.

"Too many to count," the press officer said. "It has covered three blocks...and we don't know if anybody is still alive in the area."

"That's it," the mayor said. "Call in the National Guard... and somebody close that window!"

Outside, the crazed fluting of Rickman's plasma filled the air.

People screamed.

The plasma *surged*.

It took thirty minutes to muster the National Guard. In

that time, the plasma spread by five blocks in every direction.

If there was a noise, it consumed whatever made it. Trucks, people, dogs and subway cars, all fell under the surging protoplasm, and all served to feed its exponential growth.

The National Guard brought in jeeps.

The plasma ate them.

They brought in choppers.

The plasma ate them, protoplasmic tendrils shooting skyward to suck the machines out of the air.

The Guard used bazookas.

The plasma *surged*, and suddenly, the Guard was gone.

The city was full of noise.

The plasma fed.

The president got involved twenty minutes later. Assembled in his room were the chief of staff, the head of Homeland Security and the director of the FBI.

"So what is it doing now?" the president asked.

"Still growing," the head of Homeland Security answered. "And still feeding." He was white as a sheet and trembling.

"How many casualties?" the president whispered.

"Too many to count," the chief of staff said. "It has taken most of New York State, and we don't know if anybody is still alive in the area. It will be here in minutes."

"That's it," the president said. "Call in the Air Force. We're going to nuke it...and somebody shut that window!"

Outside, the crazed fluting of Rickman's plasma filled the air.

• • •

The plasma lay along the eastern seaboard covering most of New York and New Jersey.

Flocks of birds cawed and fluttered.

The plasma ate them.

Three passenger jets inward bound from Europe passed overhead at thirty thousand feet.

The plasma threw up tendrils and ate them.

The bomber carrying the nuke came in at over a thousand miles per hour.

The plasma ate it.

The nuke exploded creating a fireball of white heat and radiation at more than a million degrees centigrade.

The plasma ate it, *surged,* and headed for Canada.

The president of the European Union got involved an hour later. Assembled in his room were the heads of the UK, France and Germany. The president of Russia was on a TV screen, linked in by satellite.

"So what is it doing now?" the president of the EU asked.

"Still growing," the Russian president answered. "And still feeding." He was white as a sheet and trembling.

"How many casualties?" the president whispered.

"Too many to count," the Prime Minister of the UK said. "It has covered most of North America and is heading south and east fast...and we don't know if anybody is still alive anywhere. It will be here in minutes."

"We only have one option," the president said. We hit it with every missile NATO and Russia have and hope for the best. And somebody close that window!"

Outside, the crazed fluting of Rickman's plasma filled the air.

• • •

Over a thousand nuclear weapons were launched in the next fifteen minutes...enough firepower to start, or finish, a global war, enough mega-tonnage to destroy every city on the planet.

The plasma ate them all and *surged.*

The last human beings on the planet got involved an hour later. Assembled in a lab at the South Pole were scientists from the US, Brazil, France and Germany.

"So what is it doing now?" the Brazilian asked.

"Still growing," the head scientist answered. "And still feeding." He was white as a sheet and trembling.

"Is there anybody left?" someone whispered.

"I doubt it," the Frenchman said. "The last we heard it had covered the rest of the planet and was heading south fast."

"We only have one option," the head scientist said. "We keep quiet, and hope it passes."

The crazed fluting of Rickman's plasma filled the air.

The scientists sat in silence, barely breathing.

Their generator kicked in noisily.

The plasma *surged.*

TWIST

Daniel Pyle

Del poked at the rubble with a length of twisted metal that might once have been a sign post or part of a barbed-wire fence. For all he knew, it had come from a hundred miles away. He'd found it in the shredded ruins of what had once been the master bedroom.

He sifted through a mound of sheetrock, found a microwave door and a plunger. He overturned a splintered end table and uncovered a nest of torn magazines and paperback books. To the east, between him and the sun, a single jag of wall with a stump of chimney jutted into the sky, casting a shadow across the debris and piles of ruined possessions. He stayed clear of it, afraid it might fall at any second, though part of him wanted to go sit beneath it and wait for it to come crashing down on his head and end this nightmare.

He surveyed the surrounding countryside. There were no neighbors within sight, but there were plenty of uprooted trees and windblown bits of garbage. The tornado had left a mile-wide scar through the region, had destroyed hundreds of homes and millions of dollars worth of property, but out here in the middle of nowhere, it was hard to remember that the twister hadn't targeted his home specifically, come down from the heavens with the sole purpose of spinning his world away.

When Jackson slapped his catcher's mitt of a hand on Del's shoulder, Del jumped and nearly shrieked.

"Sorry," Jackson said. And Del knew he was apologizing for more than just startling him. *I'm sorry about your house*, he was saying. *And your things. And your family, of course.*

Del waved the word away half-heartedly but couldn't bring himself to look the big man in the face.

"We'll find them," Jackson said. "I truly believe that."

Del nodded, tried to respond, and couldn't find the words. He spun the band on his left ring finger and focused every bit of his energy on not breaking down.

What Jackson hadn't said, what neither of them could bring themselves to say out loud, was that if they *did* find them, it would probably be in a field somewhere between here and Missouri, pulled apart by the twister, dead.

A lump formed in his throat. He turned away from his friend and let out a single, loud sob. He felt a fresh wave of tears coming and could do nothing to stop it, so he sat down on the remains of a closet door and let himself cry. Jackson sat beside him, wrapped an arm around his shoulders, and said nothing.

When Del had cried himself dry (not for the first time that day, and probably not for the last), he wiped his face on the crook of his arm and stood. Jackson, also standing, clapped him on the back, and Del gave him a trembling half-smile.

Jackson's house and family had come through the storm relatively unscathed. They'd lost a couple of tree limbs and a few shingles off their roof. Nothing more. Del wanted to hate the man, curse his good fortune, but it was hard to hate someone who'd stayed up all night helping you dig through the disaster that had once been your home, and you could hardly blame a guy for being lucky. Hell, half the town and surrounding farmland looked like it had never been within a million miles of a tornado.

Del went back to searching, looking for anything worth finding, anything that had made it through, telling himself he *wasn't* looking for body parts, convincing himself that his wife and kids had made it out in time, had driven to a neighbor's when they heard the sirens, someone with a storm shelter, someone with safety.

But if that were true, where were they now? Why hadn't they come home (if you could call it home)? Why wasn't he holding them in his arms?

He'd tried to call Jen's cell a hundred times, had tried for hours straight. But the calls never went through. Every circuit in the area was overloaded. Thousands of people looking for loved ones, wanting to check in or volunteer to help. Thousands more just wanting to know what had happened. Telephone gawkers. Del doubted you'd be able to make a reliable phone call for many days to come. Maybe weeks.

He imagined his family huddled together in a basement or a storm shelter somewhere. Jen with her arms wrapped around their daughters. Dani, a six-year-old doll with eyes and hair almost the exact same shade of golden brown. Lucy, two years younger, blonde and rosy cheeked and equally beautiful. He wondered if they'd gotten trapped, stuck beneath a relocated barn or a blown-over tree. Maybe they were digging their way out right now. Or trying to.

Maybe.

He kicked over a cracked toilet. Water spilled out of the overturned tank and onto a strip of wood that might have been roof decking or a chunk of cheap cabinetry.

He turned back into the rubble. Half the items he came across had never belonged to his family. He found papers and receipts from counties away, bits of toys and lawn furniture that could have come from anywhere. He supposed there were other people looking at similar messes, maybe picking up bits and pieces of Del's worldly goods, wondering briefly where they'd come from before tossing them back among the detritus.

"I should have been here," Del said.

Jackson sat on an exposed section of foundation, drinking from one of the two bottles of Gatorade they'd brought with them. "What?"

"If I'd been here, maybe—"

"Come on, man," Jackson said and stood up. "Don't waste your energy thinking that kind of shit. If you'd been here, you'd be d...you'd be missing too." He capped his Gatorade and put it down on the foundation next to Del's.

Del didn't have to ask what word Jackson had almost said. *Dead.* That's what he'd been thinking, what he was no doubt thinking still. If Del had been here, he'd be dead. Just like the hundreds of others sucked into the sky.

Del thought about the suitcase in Jackson's guest bedroom, the one with the airline tags still fastened around the handle. He'd only been gone for the weekend. There were two changes of clothes in that bag, a few toiletries, a pair of stuffed tigers he'd brought back for the girls, and an iPad. As he moved through the surrounding heaps, he tried not to consider that those few items might be all he had left in the world.

"Hey!" Jackson said and waved his arms. "Over here! I hear something moving."

His heart thumped. "What is it?"

Jackson flipped over a twisted sheet of plastic and glass that Del realized had once been their television. Jackson stared down into the junk and rubbed his eyes. "What in the world is this?"

Del frowned and waded toward his friend.

The once-television had been covering a deep depression

in the ruins, a hollow the size of

(a little girl's bed)

a coffee table. At the bottom of this indention lay something Del first mistook for a ratty blue bath towel.

"I don't—"

The towel moved. It separated into three segments, and then one of the pieces opened its eyes and looked up at them.

"Jesus Christ!" Jackson fell back on his ass.

Although Del managed to stay on his feet, he took a giant step away from the pit.

What the hell?

The thing (things?) in the rubble mewled. The sound reminded him of a cat. But more chittery. Like a parrot *imitating* a cat.

Del forced himself to take a deep breath and stepped back toward the hole.

"What is it?" Jackson asked, still sitting on his butt, a sheaf of waterlogged papers beneath him.

Del stared into the cavity.

There were three of the things. About the size of kittens. Their fur looked blue, but Del thought the color might be a reflection of the sky, that the things' fur might actually be clear, or at least very pale white.

Reflective fur? Was that possible?

They had flat faces and big, buggy eyes.

"I have no idea what they are," Del said. "But there are three of them."

One of the three lay very still. Del could see its left eye, glossy and bulging.

"I think one of them is dead."

Jackson pushed himself up, almost falling again when the papers shifted beneath him. He moved beside Del and craned his neck.

"Are they cats?"

"I don't think so," Del said. "At least not any kinds of cats I've ever seen."

The things had no visible ears, and when one of them rolled onto its side, it revealed a row of thin legs protruding from its belly. Dozens of them. Like caterpillar legs. The creature thrashed and flipped on its back. Long loops of bright-red guts spilled out of a wound on its belly. It flailed its legs, grabbing at the innards with tiny, almost invisible fingers at the end of each limb.

"That one's hurt bad," Jackson said.

Del nodded. He wanted to turn away before he puked, but he couldn't make himself stop watching.

Jackson stepped away from the hole. Del listened to him rummage through the debris but never took his eyes off the creatures. When Jackson came back, he was holding a tattered plastic shower curtain.

"This was all I could find."

"For what?"

Jackson gestured toward the animals. "Whatever that thing is, it's in some serious pain."

As if to confirm this, the creature cried out again. A long, reverberating wail.

Del finally shifted his attention fully away from the creatures. He eyed Jackson and the wadded curtain. "You want to kill it?"

Jackson huffed. "I don't *want* to, but it's the right thing to do, don't you think? Put it out of its misery?"

Del turned back to the creature. More of its intestines had fallen out. For every loop it pulled back into its body, two more spilled onto the surrounding debris.

"You're right," Del said and held out his hand.

Jackson didn't hand him the curtain. "It's okay," he said. "I'll do it. You shouldn't—"

"No. I'll do it. It's my house. Or what's left of it. Give me the curtain." He waggled his fingers.

Jackson handed the curtain over, and Del spread it out flat on the ground beside the hole. He grabbed the still creature first. When he lifted it, its head flopped bonelessly to the side. Dead for sure. It didn't stink yet and hadn't stiffened, so Del guessed it probably hadn't been dead long. He wondered where it had come from, how long the storm had whipped it around before depositing it on his property.

When his shadow fell over the dead creature, it lost its blue hue. Its fur *was* a pale, milky white. Del could see a Picassoesque reflection of his face in the matted hide.

He found an unripped section of shower curtain and laid the creature on it.

"I'm sorry," he whispered.

He reached back into the depression for the gutted creature. It grabbed his hand when he tried to pick it up, and he almost pulled back, but its limbs and fingers were soft, almost whiskery. It didn't seem to have either the ability or the desire to hurt him. Still, he kept his fingers away from its mouth. You never knew what an injured animal might do. Especially if the animal happened to be a mysterious, cryptozoological non-animal with no business anywhere outside a Ray Bradbury story.

When he pulled the thing out of the hole, its guts spilled out onto his hand and wrist. The bloody coils were warm, sticky. Del placed the second creature beside the first, brushed the innards off his hand and into a pile between the animals.

Jackson had moved around the hole to study the creatures.

"This is some weird-ass shit," he said. "You ever seen anything like this?"

Del shook his head.

"They're like aliens or something. You think they could be aliens?"

"I doubt it," Del said. "Probably just mutations."

"Mutated from what?"

Del shrugged and turned back to the hole.

At first, he thought the third creature might be okay. It didn't have any obvious wounds anyway. But when he tried to lift it out of the hole, he realized it was buried halfway in the rubble, and when he dug the debris out from around it, he found that it had been cut almost entirely in half by a triangular piece of corrugated metal. How it hadn't already bled to death, Del had no idea. He figured pulling out the metal would probably kill the thing, but he didn't see what choice he had. It was a goner either way, and leaving it there to suffer would have been even crueler.

He grabbed the metal, tugged it free, and winced when the creature let loose a long, agonized screech. Blood spurted out of its halved body.

"I'm sorry," Del said again and quickly moved the thing from the hole to the shower curtain.

"Fucking tornados," Jackson said.

Del nodded. He guessed that was as close to a eulogy as the creatures were going to get. He gathered up the edges of the curtain and formed a small sack. He squeezed out the air and then held the curtain shut as tightly as he could, so tight his fingers began to turn red and tremble.

The curtain was clear but frosted; he could see the vague shapes of the animals inside but couldn't make out their faces as he suffocated them.

He was glad for that.

He held the curtain shut for several minutes, long past the point when the creatures stopped moving. When Jackson told him that was probably good enough, he held it shut for another minute just to make sure. He counted to sixty in his head and then loosened his grip.

"We should bury them," Del said.

"Later," Jackson said. "Right now, we need—"

"We should bury them," Del repeated.

Jackson pursed his lips and said okay.

They used the bloodstained piece of corrugated metal to dig a shallow grave beneath a tree at the far end of the property. Del lowered the whole bundle—shower curtain and all—into the hole and pushed dirt on top with his bare hands.

"All right," Jackson said. "Back to it." His eyes were bloodshot and the skin beneath bagged. Del didn't wear a watch, and he couldn't check the time on his cell because he'd killed the battery trying to call Jen, but he guessed it must be at least nine in the morning. If that was true, it meant the two of them had been awake for over twenty-four hours.

"No," Del said. "You need to go home and sleep."

"Fuck that. I'm not going anywhere."

Del said, "I appreciate that, but you've got to get some rest."

"What about you? I'm not leaving you here." He crossed his massive arms over his chest, but Del could see the conflicting emotions in his face: the desire to stay here and help, be a dutiful friend, and the need to go home and catch a few winks before he used up the last of his energy and dropped on the spot.

"I can't leave," Del said. "If they come back and..." He shook his head. "I can't leave."

"You need to sleep too."

Del wiped his dirty hands on the seat of his pants. "I know. I will."

"You'll come back to the house before you collapse out here?"

"Maybe," Del said. "Or I might just lay down in the back of the car."

They'd driven out here separately, Jackson in his beat-to-hell pickup and Del in the rental sedan.

"That's not going to do you any good. You need some sleep in a real bed. Not to mention food and a shower."

Del put his hand on Jackson's shoulder and led him away from the tiny grave. "I know," he said as they walked, "but none of that matters right now."

"It might not *seem* like it does," Jackson said, "but—"

"Just give me until tonight, okay? Come back tonight and drag me back to the house or an all-you-can-eat buffet or wherever the hell you want, but I need some more time out here."

Jackson let out a long sigh. "Okay, man. If that's what you want."

"It is."

They walked around the house, through less concentrated (though no less haphazard) piles of debris, and around a massive oak that had fallen across the driveway.

Jackson had parked with his bumper less than a foot away from the trunk. He got into the pickup, started the engine, and rolled down his window.

"Don't let yourself go crazy out here," he said. "If you're not back to the house by dinner time, I'm coming back."

Del nodded. "I'm counting on it. And be careful yourself. Don't fall asleep driving home."

"I'll do my best." He reached for the emergency brake and stopped. "Del?"

Del waited.

"We're going to find them, okay?"

Del tried to smile. "Thanks for coming out here with me. For being a friend."

Jackson nodded, put the truck in reverse, and backed down the driveway.

• • •

He's found Lucy's stuffed frog not long after Jackson left and had been carrying it around with him ever since. It was dirty and torn but otherwise okay. Del had found a few tufts of stuffing poking out through small holes and pushed them back in with his finger.

He couldn't remember where Lucy had gotten the thing, whether he and Jen or some other relative had bought it for her. He knew only that she loved it and slept with it every night. He wanted to give it to her when she got back, wanted to watch her face light up when he pulled it out from behind his back.

He spent the next several hours looking for one of Dani's toys, sifting and overturning and digging. It wouldn't do to have something for one girl and not the other. Any daddy knew that. He found a plastic tiara and an illustrated copy of *The Wizard of Oz* they sometimes read at bedtime, but the tiara was broken and the book was split down the spine and missing the second half. It struck him later that the book would have been a ridiculously thoughtless gift anyway. He did finally find an old music box Dani kept on her dresser. He didn't think it was one of her favorite things exactly, but it still worked, and he guessed it was better than nothing.

He carried the two items to a recliner he'd uncovered earlier and sat down. The cushion squished and seeped water, but he didn't particularly care. His jeans were already damp and muddy, and a little water never hurt anything.

His eyelids drooped, unbelievably heavy. The sun had slipped past the midway point in the sky and started its descent toward the western horizon. Del guessed it was probably a little bit past noon. His stomach had stopped rumbling and started twisting. He knew he'd need to eat something soon, but skipping a meal or two wasn't going to kill him. The hunger was good. The hunger had kept him awake this long.

From the recliner, he could see the spot in the back yard where they'd buried the three creatures. Later, after he'd gotten some rest, he supposed he might care more about what they had been and where they'd come from, but right now all he could think about was the way they'd cried and the reflective fur that had showed him his own, disjointed face.

He sat there staring across the yard for what must have been an hour. Maybe he fell asleep for a few minutes, although he didn't think so. All he knew for sure was that by the time he noticed the movement in the trees off to the right, his face felt sunburned and his stomach was screaming at him.

The thing in the trees moved again. Branches cracked and leaves fluttered. Del thought it might be a deer or maybe even a cow or horse that had wondered through a tornado-torn fence.

It wasn't a deer. Or a cow or a horse.

The dust devil spun out of the woods and into the back yard.

Del blinked.

The mini cyclone must have been ten or fifteen feet tall. It had picked up enough dirt and foliage to make itself visible, but you could still see right through it. Del had seen dust devils before, of course. You didn't grow up in Kansas and not see at least a few in your lifetime, but usually the things were smaller and spun out of existence before you could get a really good look at them. This one hovered in place for a full minute or more before zigging toward the lone wall still pointing into the sky and then zagging back across the property.

It moved toward the tree (what Del had started to think of as the burial tree) and the small mound of dirt beneath.

The dust devil whirred above the mini grave, picking up more dirt and getting darker.

Del sat forward in the wet recliner.

He wasn't seeing this. Couldn't be. He'd fallen asleep and this was all just a very weird dream. He put the stuffed frog and the music box in his lap and pinched himself on the upper thigh as hard as he could.

The pinch hurt. A lot. He rubbed his leg and hissed air through his teeth.

Across the property, a corner of the shower curtain poked out of the dirt. Then another. Del wanted to scream at the dust devil to stop it, that it was desecrating sacred ground, but that was insane. The whole situation was insane.

More of the curtain appeared, and then suddenly the entire thing flew into the air, spinning within the cyclone, flapping like a flag in a high wind. From this distance and as dark as the dust devil had gotten, Del couldn't tell for sure, but he thought he saw three pale shapes twisting inside the tiny tornado. If he got up and ran across the yard, would he see the three creatures in there? He thought he might, but it didn't matter. He wasn't going to get up, and it was too late anyway. As quickly as it had come, the dust devil disappeared. It zipped across the yard, carrying the twisted shower curtain with it, and spun back into the woods.

Del waited for a few minutes, trying to convince himself that he'd been imagining things, that he was sleep deprived and a bit delirious, before getting up and crossing the back yard. He carried the frog and the music box with him, clutched to his chest.

Beneath the burial tree, he found a hole, a lot of swirled dirt, and nothing else. The shower curtain was gone. And the three dead creatures with it.

He turned to the trees where the dust devil had disappeared, looked back at the hole, then finally shook his head and walked toward the car.

Sleep. He had to get some sleep. Maybe this would all make a little more sense when he woke up.

Then again, maybe it wouldn't.

He opened the rental's back door and climbed inside. He turned the key on the bottom of the music box and put the box down on the floorboard. He curled up on the seat, hugging Lucy's frog.

Dani's music box tinkled. Then sleep swooped in and overtook him.

The roar that woke him sounded like a revving engine. It came closer and got louder, more like an approaching train.

Del blinked his eyes and straightened his stiff back. He wasn't sure how long he'd been sleeping, but it had definitely gotten darker outside. Not quite night yet, but getting there for sure.

He sat up, still holding Lucy's frog, wondering if he was hearing Jackson's grumbling truck but simultaneously doubting that even a truck in serious need of a new muffler could make that much noise.

He turned around in his seat and looked through the back windshield.

The tornado filled half the sky. It churned at the bottom, plucking trees from the ground and sucking them into its black, spinning body. It rose into the dark, monstrous clouds swirling through the sky above, at least a mile wide at the base, probably two times that wide at the top.

Del sucked in a ragged breath and felt bursts of adrenaline course through his body.

Another tornado? It couldn't be. Did the universe really hate him this much?

His first worthwhile thought was that he should slip into the driver's seat and put the pedal to the metal. But it was too late for that. The tornado had already reached FR 125 less than half a mile to the west, and it was moving fast. He might be able to back out of the driveway before the cyclone reached him, but he'd get no farther than that.

He knew he ought to get out of the car, find a ditch or some other hollow to lie low in until the twister passed, but there were no ditches out here, no valleys or stream beds. The land spread out flat and wide for miles.

And if the car couldn't outdrive the tornado, he sure as hell couldn't outrun it.

He guessed the only option left was to get into the footwell, cover his head, and pray.

He lifted Dani's music box off the floor and contorted his body into the space between the front and back seats. Then he covered his head and neck as best he could, knowing it probably wouldn't do any good, that a tornado that size would suck the car right off the ground and put it down miles away in dozens of pieces.

Something slapped against the windshield. He turned his head, peeked through his arms and saw a broken section of billboard sporting most of the red and blue Pepsi logo. The billboard slipped up the windshield, pulled away, and disappeared into the sky.

Del trembled and wrapped his arms more tightly around his head.

By the time the tornado reached him, the car was shaking and bouncing and the noise had reached deafening levels. A second object slammed into the windshield and cracked the glass, but Del didn't bother looking to see what had done the damage. He tried to push himself under the front seats, though there was nowhere near enough room and it probably wouldn't have done him any good anyway.

The car rocked from side to side, back and forth. It lifted off the ground and slammed back down with enough force to pop Del up onto the back seat. He scrambled back into the footwell and screamed.

The car lifted again, but it didn't drop this time. It spun into the sky and flipped end over end. Del flew up against the roof and then over the backs of the front seats and into the steering column. His back hit the steering wheel, and his head crunched into the driver-side window. The combination of impacts sent jolts of pain through most of his body. He fell sideways across the front seats. The gearshift punched into his side, and he heard a crack he thought must have been one of his ribs.

Something broke through the back window, tore off the headrest inches from Del's face, and continued through the front windshield. It looked like part of a telephone pole. Safety glass fell across his body and pattered against the dashboard, and the screaming winds got louder still.

Del lifted his head just enough to see the pole shoot through the sky ahead and then splinter when another gust of wind caught it from the side and snapped it in half.

The hole in the windshield sucked at him like a vacuum. He wrapped his arms around the back of the driver's seat and held on for dear life.

The car flipped again, this time the opposite way, and Del ended up back in the back seat. He scrambled for something to hold on to. He found a seatbelt and thought about trying to buckle himself in. But he didn't think his shaking hands would cooperate. Instead, he wrapped the belt around his arm half a dozen times and tied it tight, cutting off circulation to his hand, not caring.

Something smacked the back door and left a basketball-sized indentation. More safety glass rained down across his head.

Del tried to keep himself low, out of the way of any further projectiles, but every time the car spun or lurched, he ended up back on top of the seat, sometimes sitting up, sometimes upside down and staring into the footwell.

He'd lost the frog and the music box, although he didn't remember it happening. He supposed they might still be in the car somewhere, maybe in the front seat, but it was probably more likely that they'd gotten sucked through a window. It didn't matter, of course, they were just inanimate things, but somehow losing them felt like a failure.

He clutched the seatbelt and screamed again.

Something fluttered outside the window. He barely saw it at first and thought it must be a bed sheet or a sun-bleached tarp, but when it flapped its enormous, membranous wings and flew closer to the window, Del got a better look.

The creature had half a dozen knobby legs curling out of a segmented, ant-like body. Its head was pointed and insectile, and the huge black sockets on either side looked withered and dead. It unhinged its jaw like a snake and revealed an unnaturally huge mouth full of rows and rows of tiny, jagged teeth. He had no way of knowing for sure, but he thought it must have had a wingspan of at least five feet.

Del knew then that he must have died, that he was in Hell and this winged thing was his own personal demon tormentor.

The car stopped spinning for a second, and Del could see more of the creatures in the distance, flitting through the cyclone, darting around speeding debris, pumping their wings and climbing up or folding them in and diving down. He saw one creature with a litter of kitten-sized, caterpillar-like things clinging to its chest—maybe feeding, maybe just holding on for the ride—and coughed out a bile-flavored breath.

The beast outside the rental's window flapped its wings again. For just a second, Del thought he could see his reflection in its belly and chest. Then it turned, and the reflection disappeared.

A second creature flew in behind the first. It held a bundle in its spindly arms. Del thought it looked like something wrapped in a frosted shower curtain. But that couldn't be, could it? What were the chances that—

And that was when the car came to a sudden, jolting stop and folded in around Del.

He could barely hear the sounds of the screeching metal and breaking glass against the tornado. The seatbelt kept him tethered to the back seat but could do nothing about the crumpling roof. It hit the back of his head and knocked him onto the seat. He hit face first and felt his nose break. As blood spilled across his mouth and chin, he thought he saw one of the flying beasts diving toward the jagged hole that had once been a window frame, and then he fell back on the seat and lost consciousness.

When he opened his eyes, the sky had cleared. He saw a sliver of it through the gap between the car's roof and the tops of the back seats.

He was in a narrow, cocoon-like space. the steering wheel and dashboard had shifted into the front seats and pushed everything back toward the trunk. The back seat was mostly intact, and he could see a few inches of floorboard between it and the rearranged front.

Blood pooled in his mouth. He turned his head to the side and spat it out. His arm ached. When he looked at it, he saw a hand so bluish-purple it was almost black. He untied the seatbelt and hoped it wasn't too late, that he hadn't killed off the hand.

Before he tried to get up, he tested his arms, legs, and neck. There was plenty of pain, but nothing seemed broken except his nose and maybe a few ribs. He pushed up on his elbow, winced at the throbbing ache in his side, and finally managed to turn himself onto his belly.

Blood dripped out of his nose and across the bits of glass in the footwell. He ran his good hand across his nostrils. His other hand had started to tingle. He guessed that was a good thing, but the sensation just about drove him crazy. For a minute, all he could do was cradle the hand to his chest and try to ignore the pins and needles.

When he thought he could manage it, he pushed up on his forearms and tried to open the car door. It squeaked open, but only an inch or so before hitting something outside. Del certainly wasn't going to make it through that narrow crack.

He looked back over his shoulder at the other door, which was the only other obvious point of exit. He kicked at it. Nothing.

It took a series of painful movements, but he was finally able to turn himself and wrap his fingers around the door handle. He pulled on it and pushed the door with his shoulder.

It squeaked and moved the tiniest fraction of an inch.

He pushed harder, strained until he thought he might pass out again.

With a single metallic *pop*, the door swung open and fell away from the car, free from its hinges. Del followed it, crawling out of the car and flopping onto his back.

Tree limbs swayed overhead, mostly stripped of their leaves, littered with bits of paper, cloth, wood, and other unrecognizable materials.

Del lay there for several minutes, not sure where he was and not caring, only happy to be alive and relatively uninjured.

He saw the sun through a gap in the trees. It had found the horizon and turned a dark shade of red-orange. A few clouds floated above, and a whole bank of them sped eastward, but the sky to the west looked clear and peaceful.

Del decided he ought to try to get up and figure out where he was, find some civilization, a hospital. Being careful with his ribs, he got to his knees and then to his feet.

He wobbled, almost fell, and caught himself on the trunk of the totaled rental sedan, which had come to rest wedged between two trees. The front half looked like it had run into a brick wall at a thousand miles an hour.

Del couldn't believe he'd lived through this. The crash should have pulped him.

When he regained his balance, he took his weight off the car and walked through the trees. He had no idea where the nearest road might be, how many miles from his home the tornado had carried him. If he'd known whether he was north or south of I-70, he guessed he could have found the interstate eventually, but he didn't. All he could do was start walking until he saw something he recognized or came across a road or house.

He pushed through a pair of dense bushes. The trees opened up ahead. He saw a fringe of undergrowth and a field of alfalfa beyond that. He stumbled out of the woods, looking for a farmhouse, afraid any structure he found would be demolished and lifeless.

But before he could spot a house (or the remains of one), he saw something else in the field ahead. It flapped in the breeze.

A shower curtain.

Del remembered the creatures he'd seen inside the tornado. They'd been figments of his imagination, had to have been, but he recalled one holding a curtain-wrapped bundle in its monstrous arms. Like a gift. Or a newborn baby.

He approached the curtain one hesitant step after another. It lay in a section of field the tornado had beaten flat, like a crop circle. Beneath the curtain: three, unmoving lumps, one adult sized and the other two smaller. A stuffed frog sat atop the shower curtain on one of the smaller mounds, and a music box lay slightly off-kilter on the other.

Del dropped to his knees a few steps shy of the shower curtain and wailed. He got down on his hands and cried into the torn and uprooted alfalfa. When his wobbly arms wouldn't support him anymore, he laid himself down and flipped onto his back.

He sobbed, stared at the blurry sky overhead, and listened to the shower curtain flap in the dying wind.

WILD RELEASE

Keith Gouveia

"Go go go!" Ray Torres shouted as his men frantically chopped down trees and cleared underbrush. "I need an ETA on the water tankers. You there! Get that bulldozer out of the way. We need to get this backfire going. Hustle!"

The forest was an eclectic combination of coniferous and broad-leaved trees, numerous species of fungi, ferns, and shrubs. Plenty of fuel for a raging fire.

He felt guilty simply directing his men when they had been going non-stop for six hours, doing their very best to combat the encroaching forest fire. The blaze—ignited by three, bored teenagers already in custody—had consumed twenty percent of the forest surrounding the Great Lakes and was threatening the Canadian border. If they couldn't get control of it, the raging fire would garner natural disaster status. Firefighters from both countries worked together to fight back the wildfire before it caused further damage.

I'll be damned if this fire is going to break into Wisconsin, Ray thought.

The animals were already making their exit by the time the firefighters drew a stop-line in the undergrowth. White-tailed deer, wolves, black bears, and moose passed by, united by a single threat, panic in their eyes.

We've got to stop this.

Something rustled in a nearby bush. Probably an animal,

trapped and scared. Ray took his eyes off his men and looked toward the noise.

"Don't worry little guy," he said in a soft tone. "We're here to help. There's still time to get out."

"Captain, we're ready," said one of his men, Joshua. "Water tanker is five minutes away."

"All right." He looked away from the bush, hunched over, and picked up a branch to use as kindling. "Let's do this before it's too late."

He used a flip-top lighter to ignite the branch. The leaves sizzled and glowed orange.

"Let's hope this is enough," Ray said and tossed the kindling onto the remaining underbrush.

A crackling sound filled the air as the flame spread outward. Ray felt heat on his face and stepped back to watch from a safer distance.

Someone screamed behind him.

"What was—"

Ray turned around in time to see two massive hands reach out from a bush near where he'd just been standing, grab hold of Joshua by the shoulders, and pull him into the underbrush.

Shrieks from the rustling bush drowned out the crackling fire.

"Joshua!" Ray called.

Several of his men hurried over. "What happened?" one of them asked.

Another fireman opened his mouth to speak but was cut off when a limbless torso flew out of the bush and landed at his feet. Blood seeped from the stumps where the extremities had been.

"Ahhh! Help me!" someone else bellowed.

Ray turned in time to see another of his men disappear into the bush.

"What the hell is that?" a veteran firefighter asked, his voice shaky.

"I don't know!"

The remaining firefighters took up their pickaxes, the only weapons they had, and gathered in a circle. With their backs to each other, they eyed the tree line. Branches shook. The ground trembled with each step the mysterious attacker took. Its heavy breaths and grunts echoed on the air, making it impossible to determine its exact location.

"Be ready," Ray said, doing his best to keep his cool.

Once more, screaming filled the air.

"Danny! It took Danny!" someone howled.

The fire at Ray's back intensified and drove back the shadows their assailant was using for cover. Ray didn't know what was stalking them, but he was certain it was no animal. It was picking them off systematically, toying with them.

Ray caught movement at his peripheral and turned left to see the silhouette of a man against the forest backdrop. But it was too large, too frightening to be human.

"What—"

The last thing Ray saw was an enormous rock slicing through the air, coming right at his head.

David Chase rolled over and peered at the alarm clock. The LCD numbers came into focus: 3:00 am.

"Who the hell—"

A violent knock at his front door cut him off.

"Sheriff. Wake up!"

Sounds like Sean, he thought.

"This better be damn important."

David huffed as he swung his feet over the edge of his bed. His toes probed the hardwood floor for his slippers, and once his feet were firmly planted within them, he stood and grabbed his robe from the door.

The hammering on his front door continued.

"Damnit, Sean. Hold on," he mumbled.

More knocks.

"I'm coming!"

"Finally," the young deputy said when David opened the door. "We've got a problem."

"What is it?"

"One of the firefighting units failed to radio in."

He peered past Sean. An orange glow pulsed on the horizon. "So? They're probably busy battling the fire."

"Maybe. But we've been asked to check it out. A water tanker was scheduled to meet up with them, but no one showed."

David sighed and said, "Did you call Tracey?"

"No sir, the lines are down. That's why I'm here."

"All right. Get your ass back to the station in case any other calls come in. I'll drive over to Tracey's, and we'll head out there together."

"You're the boss." Sean turned back toward his squad car.

"And Sean."

"Yeah?"

"Take it easy on my door next time, huh."

Sean acknowledged this with a quick flutter of his hand and kept walking. David shook his head.

On a normal day, Douglas County was peaceful and serene. The local police force of each city took care of the day-to day business while David and his deputies handled the outlying regions, which covered most of the area around the Great Lakes. His average day consisted of helping lost hikers, scaring off hunters, and patrolling rarely used roads. Though there were times he dreamt of a little action, this had never been what he had in mind.

The kids who started this are lucky they're not in my jurisdiction. I'd ring their necks.

David took a quick shower and pulled on his pale gray uniform. Then he got in his car and headed for Tracey's place. The blanket of haze reduced visibility and turned what was normally a ten or fifteen minute drive into a half hour ordeal.

All I need now is to hit a deer, he thought and squeezed the steering wheel.

He made it to Tracey's without incident and walked up to the door praying to God she didn't castrate him for disturbing her. He knocked and heard something break inside the house.

The door swung open. "Don't think you can just come... Oh, Sheriff, what are you doing here?"

He was surprised to see her still in uniform. Her eyes were red and puffy.

What have I gotten myself into?

"Sorry if this is a bad time," he said, "but duty calls."

Tracey stepped aside. "Come in. I could use the distraction. Just let me splash some water on my face." She sniffed.

Her tone caught him by surprise. He had always known her to be a strong, domineering woman and didn't remember ever seeing her cry. Inside, David noticed broken glass by the fireplace and a knocked over lamp. His gaze drifted toward the mantle.

"What happened?" he asked after realizing Tony's picture was missing. Tracey and Tony, a fellow officer, had dated for years and been engaged for two.

"Nothing," she replied and closed the door behind him. She turned and walked away, heading for the bathroom.

Okay, she obviously doesn't want to talk about it.

"You've got one of those French presses, right?" he called out, trying to change the subject.

"Yeah," she hollered back. "Make enough for two, would ya!"

"Sure."

He walked across the living room and noticed a pile of half-finished knitting in a chair.

She knits?

He flipped over the ball of yarn, saw tiny socks hanging from the knitting needles. Baby socks.

Huh.

He raised his eyebrows and walked out of the room.

As David prepared the coffee, his thoughts drifted to the missing firemen. He needed to find out what had happened, of course, but he wasn't all that thrilled with venturing into a blazing forest fire.

"Tony and I called off the engagement," Tracey said as she entered the kitchen.

The information shocked him—he thought he'd walked in on the aftermath of a lover's spat, not a serious breakup. Still, over the years he'd seen Tracey's temper, how she could overreact, and he couldn't help but wonder what she had done this time to drive Tony away.

"The tests came back." She ran a hand through her hair. "I can't have children."

David frowned. "I didn't realize you were trying."

"Yeah," she said. A tear streamed down her left cheek, and she turned away from him to wipe it off.

"I...I'm so sorry." David stepped closer to her and opened his arms. She slumped against him.

As her head found his shoulder, she breathed in deeply. A loud wheeze escaped her lips as an all out cry came over her. He held her tight, allowing her a moment. Her tears dampened his uniform. He knew her pain (or some of it anyway; the break-up part), had felt it when Lisa left him for a younger man years ago. People changed. Ideals, hopes, and dreams evolved with age, and people drifted apart. No one knew that better than him.

"You guys have been together a long time. I'm sure he'll come around," he said, although he barely believed the words himself.

"Fuck him," she said and pulled away from David. "Things were never that good with him anyway. Always had his eye out for the next best thing. I can do better. But I always dreamed about having children. To be responsible for a life. Ya know?"

"Yeah, I do."

She looked at him doubtfully, but said nothing.

"C'mon, we need to get out to the site," he said.

She sniffled and pointed over his shoulder. "I've got some travel mugs in the cupboard."

Coffee in hand, they slipped into his squad car and headed up Route 53. Though they couldn't see the smoke yet, they could smell it in the air, even some twenty miles out. On their way, they saw two airplanes release water over the affected area. By the time they arrived at the last reported coordinates of the firefighters, the sun had broken over the horizon.

"It's going to be hard to see anything out there with all this smoke," Tracey said when they'd stepped out of the car.

"I know," he said.

David popped the trunk. He kept all sorts of supplies back there: road flares, a first aid kit, folded blankets, bottles of water, extra ammo, anything he might need, compartmentalized and ready to go.

"Don't forget to grab a mask," he said. "We don't need to collapse from smoke inhalation out here."

"Here's to finding them alive," she replied. She grabbed a mask and slipped it on.

David couldn't get his mask on fast enough. The air was

thick with soot. The smell of sulfur burned his nostrils and eyes, instantly bringing tears, and he couldn't help but think what a bad idea this had been. The thought shamed him. This was his job and there was no one else to do it, but still, what good would he do anyone if he ended up trapped in or killed by the fire?

The trees and underbrush close to the road still held their vibrant green colors, but the deeper they went into the forest, the more desolate the picture became. Tree bark was scorched black, and the few remaining leaves were brown and brittle. Though it was obvious the aerial assault on the fire was working, there were still plenty of smoldering fires on the forest floor. Soon there would be nothing left to fuel them, but David kicked dirt on the flames as he passed anyway, wanting to help in any way he could. Tracey saw what he was doing and followed suit.

David glanced around him, thought about how many animals the blaze must have uprooted, and his heart sank. The forest surrounding the Great Lakes had always been a place of refuge, tranquil and serene. Now all that remained was death and decay. He wondered how long it would take the forest to heal.

"Look!" Tracey pointed up ahead.

David squinted and saw a large bulldozer. "Must be the firebreak."

"Well, what are we waiting for?" Tracey darted ahead.

David took a deep breath before running after her.

As they drew closer to the bulldozer, David noticed its yellow paint was blackened and bubbling away. But something else also caught his eye: a body, sprawled on the ground beside the machine. He picked up his pace.

"What is it?" Tracey asked as he passed her.

"Someone's...hurt." He couldn't bring himself to suggest anything worse.

He reached the body. But it wasn't just *one* body. Arms, legs, and other bloody parts decorated the ashen ground. The sight sickened him. He turned away and went back to stop Tracey before she could see the worst of it. The body—that first body—had been unidentifiable. A large rock jutted from its face, leaving nothing but broken glass from the protective mask, mangled flesh, and blood.

"Don't look," David said as loudly as he could through the mask.

Tracey peered over his shoulder despite the warning. "Oh... Jesus!"

"I told you not to look."

Her face paled. "Who is it?"

David told her he didn't know.

"They're all dead?" she asked and stepped around the faceless body.

"Looks that way."

"What did this? Animals?"

"No," he said and carefully looked over the severed appendages. "The pieces don't look chewed on or anything. Just ripped apart. We better call it in. We're going to need backup. Maybe one of the men snapped under the pressure."

Tracey examined the grounds, her color returning. "The coroner's going to have a helluva time matching up these pieces."

David radioed dispatch and filled Sean in. When Sean started asking questions, David cut him off: "Just get us some help out here asap."

"Sheriff!" Tracey shouted. "Over here!"

David released the button on his radio and walked over to Tracey. "Whatcha got?"

"Blood."

"There's blood everywhere."

"Yeah, but this is leading away. Look." She pointed to the underbrush on the unburned side of the firebreak, and David noticed a splotch of blood weighing down a leaf.

"Somebody went this way," she said. "Maybe the killer."

"Only one way to find out." He drew his gun.

Tracey followed him through the brush. The patches of blood turned to sporadic droplets as they went on, and David couldn't help but wonder if the attacker (if there *was* an attacker) was injured. Of course, maybe they weren't following a killer at all; maybe one of the firefighters had lived and run away. They might be just as likely to find another body as an ax-wielding psychopath.

"How far should we go?"

"All the way," he replied.

"What if we can't find our way back?"

"I know where we're going. I've—"

He saw something impossible sitting on a boulder ahead. It slouched on the rock, breathing heavily. Even doubled over like it was, its size was undeniable.

It can't be. It's not possible. He raised his gun.

A twig snapped as Tracey approached, and the beast turned toward them. It jumped to its feet and roared.

Standing there—over eight feet tall, covered head to toe with dark, reddish hair—was an enormous creature, almost man-like but so very different. Its large eyes stared out from beneath its ridged brow and large, low-set forehead. It had a gigantic head with a single crest bone running lengthwise along the midline like a gorilla's. The beast's lips and chin seemed to blend together and protrude past the upper jaw. Its teeth were short, blunt.

The creature pounded its chest with boulder-sized fists and let loose another mighty roar, but it had a glint of fear in its eyes. David couldn't imagine what a creature like this could possibly be afraid of.

"Ho...holy shit."

The beast stepped forward and winced in pain. David squinted and saw blood matting the creature's fur, red on red. A ragged edge clearly defined the open wound in its upper thigh.

With her gun at her side, Tracey stepped past David and whispered, "You need to lower your weapon."

"Are you crazy?"

The beast grunted and took another step toward them.

"No," she said. "Back up slowly. Don't make any sudden moves that it could take as a threat."

David trembled with fear, but Tracey seemed unafraid. She was calm, collected, a far cry from the sobbing mess she'd been when he knocked on her door earlier that morning.

Did she know about this?

He stared at her.

The beast charged unexpectedly, and David pointed his gun. With little time to aim, he fired a warning shot. The beast stopped and ducked. Tracey screamed and put herself between David and the creature.

"What are you doing? Get out of the way!"

"You can't do this," she said.

The beast fled.

David felt a rush of adrenaline and shoved Tracey aside. "Get out of my way. We can't let it get away."

With each stride of the beast's long legs, the distance between it and David grew. Despite its size, the creature moved with elegance and grace, carefully sidestepping trees and hopping low bushes.

David raised his pistol and waited for a clear shot. He knew if he didn't do something soon, the beast would lose him and continue to roam free, to kill.

The creature veered to its right to avoid a low branch.

"Gotcha!" David pulled the trigger. The thing roared and grabbed at its side but continued to run, not looking back.

"Stop, David!" Tracey called from behind.

"You saw what it did. We have a responsibility to protect people."

He continued to chase the beast, and though the creature hadn't dropped despite the gunshot wound, it *was* slowing down. David lined up another shot and fired. The beast shifted to the left, and dirt puffed into the air as the bullet hit the ground in front of it.

"Please!"

He ignored Tracey, kept running, and aimed again. The next shot would be the one; he was sure of it. With the back of the beast's head in his sights, he fired.

The bullet hit its mark. The beast bellowed and fell to the forest floor, but it still didn't stop trying to get away. Down on all fours, it pulled itself onward. David approached the fallen giant, his gun raised, his finger on the trigger.

"David. Stop!" A gunshot boomed, and David turned around slowly, hands pointing toward the sky.

"What are you doing, Tracey?"

"You can't kill it," she said, stepping up to him.

"The hell I can't. You saw what it did. It's dangerous."

"Look out!"

Instinctively, David ducked to the ground. A large rock flew over his head. Tracey tried to avoid the projectile, but it struck her in the shoulder and knocked her to the ground. Without checking on his deputy, David whirled around. The beast was preparing to throw another rock. He fired again. The bullet struck a neighboring tree and sent splinters into the air. The creature, maybe rethinking its rocks-beat-guns offensive, dropped the stone and ran.

You're not getting away! David thought as he pursued once more. *Wonder how much money I can get for the carcass? In-*

disputable proof an urban legend exists, I could rake in a for-tune.

He realized his greed was superseding his sense of jus-tice and duty, and he didn't care. As he chased the beast, he couldn't help but wonder what other myths might be real; unicorns, leprechauns, the Loch Ness monster, all of them? Then his mind changed gears as he thought about all the things he could buy with the tabloid money. A new car. Beachfront property. Hell, maybe he couldn't satisfy Lisa the way a twenty-something could, but he'd be able to buy her enough toys to compensate.

She'll come crawling back, he thought and grinned.

He could only imagine how the devilish smile on his face must have looked when he neared the beast and fired two more rounds at it.

Both missed.

The creature zigzagged through the woods and then stopped suddenly, as if it had lost its bearings. David skid-ded to a halt as it whirled around and stared down at him. Its large arms dangled at its waist. Its chest rose and fell with each gasping breath. David took that moment to catch his own breath, keeping a safe distance. His arms trembled as he raised his gun. He was afraid any shot he fired would go wild.

The beastly almost-man broke the stare with David and glanced over its shoulder. David seized the opportunity and fired a single shot. The hot lead hit its mark, dead center of the thing's throat. The creature howled as blood gushed out of the bullet hole and cascaded down its chest. It clutched its throat with its sausage-like fingers and dropped to its knees.

As David approached, he kept his gun aimed at the crea-ture's head. The thing looked at him with large, pleading eyes. Shallow pools of tears threatened to spill down its hairy face. The beast looked over its shoulder once more. Blood gushed from its throat. Curious, David followed the beast's line of sight and noticed a cave barely visible among the trees.

It's trying to get home.

And then he had another, much more exciting thought: *Are there more of them?*

As if reading David's thoughts, the beast released its grip on the wound and let loose a gurgly roar. When it reached out for him, David shot it point blank in the center of its forehead. The creature collapsed, blood spraying out behind it and soaking the ground. David stood there and watched the body quiver.

Seconds became minutes. David exhaled and stepped over the behemoth.

He looked toward the cave.

It must've been protecting something.

The sun's rays penetrated deep into the cave's opening, but revealed none of its mysteries. David walked away from the corpse and through the trees.

As he stepped into the cave, he heard a faint sound. He stopped and listened.

Is that...crying?

He moved deeper into the beast's den, clutching his gun, finger wrapped around the trigger. Ten yards in, or maybe twenty, just as he was starting to think he would run out of light, he stumbled over a rock and almost stepped on two small creatures. They huddled together in a large nest of dried grass and torn litter, weeping. They were the size of human toddlers, but otherwise similar to the giant he had gunned down. Their eyes were closed and their gums tooth-less. Just babies.

He looked around for another adult. If there was one parent, there could be more.

But if there was, it wasn't nearby. He didn't see or hear anything besides the babies.

He stared at them for a long time. The adult's corpse was going to make him a fortune, and he wondered what he could get for one of the babies. Or for both of them. He raised his gun, pointed it at the pair of crying infants, and pulled the trigger halfway back.

He hesitated and finally took his finger off the trigger.

Don't think about it, just do it. Never mind the money. They're monsters, wild creatures, future killers. I have to do this. It's my duty.

He cocked the gun's hammer.

A gunshot echoed in the tight quarters, and David felt searing pain in his lower back. Blood poured down his side and leg. His grip on his pistol faltered, and the weapon fell to the ground as he turned around to face his assailant.

"I can't let you hurt them, David. I'm sorry."

"You...why?" he managed to say.

She shook her head. "They're not monsters. The mother might have killed those men, might have thought they were trying to burn her out, but she was only doing what I thought I'd never get the chance to do...until now."

Her finger tightened around the trigger, and David was consumed by darkness.

WHITEOUT

Danielle Bourdon

"...whiteout conditions continue for the twenty-fourth straight day..."

Jeremy Buckle fiddled with the knob on his shortwave radio, trying to get better reception. The hiss of static made it difficult to hear any news.

"Any luck?" Jo asked from the office doorway. She had changed into pajamas and pulled her hair back for the night.

"Not really. It's the same thing they've been reporting for a week." He sat back in his chair and raked a hand through his hair. Tension made his shoulders tight.

"Well there has to be *something*—"

"Jo, there's *not*. No news about any deliveries. No news about how they're going to clear the god-forsaken roads. No news, period."

"They can't expect us to starve to death," she hissed, glancing over her shoulder to the living room where the kids were playing.

"I don't know what to tell you," he said, spreading his hands in the air for emphasis. "I'm sure they didn't expect some freak series of storms to obliterate the entire country, either."

"This is Los Angeles. Surely they're better prepared—"

"Anaheim Hills, baby, if you want to get technical. And how the hell are they supposed to be prepared for *this*? It barely *rains* here, much less snows." Even to his own ears, the caustic words sounded harsh. When she pinched the bridge of her nose—a clear indication a rant was forthcoming—Jeremy got up and crossed the room. He squeezed her shoulder, trying to head off another argument.

"We only have enough food for maybe three more days, Jeremy."

To hear it put in plain words drove the pressure to provide for his family to new heights. "I know, I know—"

"I mean, you and I haven't had a decent meal in more than a week. All the stores have been cleaned out, and no trucks can get through with supplies. What the hell are we going to do? Ask the neighbors to give us supplies we've already shared and divided between us?"

"They have kids to feed, too. If we're running low, so are the rest of them."

"Maybe we should have kept what we had to ourselves." Jo seemed torn between fear and bitterness.

"You wouldn't be able to see the other kids go hungry anymore than you would let ours go hungry," he said, kneading her shoulders with gentle pressure. "I'll tell you what. Since it's already so late, I'll go see Ed in the morning. We'll figure out what to do."

"Are you sure it's safe? We couldn't even see the end of our driveway this morning."

"I'll use the rope. If I have something to follow back to our porch, I'll be fine. Ed only lives right next door."

Relenting, Jo said, "All right."

"At least we still have power. Things would be a lot worse if we—"

As if Fate were listening, the lights blinked out.

"...shit." Jeremy released her. "I'll get the flashlights."

"And a few candles," she said, turning to cross into the living room.

Jeremy felt his way like a blind man over to a cabinet in the office that held their supplies. He fished out a pair of flashlights, stuck one in his pocket, and thumbed the button on the other. A spear of illumination cut through the shadows. Already he could hear Lila, his middle child, start to fret and worry. She'd always been afraid of the dark.

"Daddy's got the flashlights, Lila."

"Hurry, there's monsters in the corner!" Lila shouted.

"Monsters aren't *real.*" Haley, four years old going on ten, set her sister straight.

"Hey Mom, I've got that old werewolf mask from Halloween. I could—"

"No honey, not now." Jo dissuaded Andrew, their eight-year-old son, from freaking Lila out completely.

Any other time, Jeremy might have smiled. If they weren't almost out of food, if there wasn't a radical storm blanketing the country, and if they hadn't just lost power, he might have found their typical banter amusing. All he could manage to feel was a fresh surge of fear. With no heat, they were going to struggle to stay warm on top of everything else.

He picked up a fat candle and was just about to tuck it under his arm when the front door crashed inward with a thunderous bang.

Lila and Haley screamed.

Startled, Jeremy whirled out of the office and ran toward the living room. Three dark silhouettes blurred through the flashlight beam. With the pistol locked upstairs in the master closet and no time to retrieve it, Jeremy cocked his arm back to pitch the candle like a missile. Before he could release it, he found himself staring down the menacing barrel of a shotgun.

"Don't make me do it," the intruder said, tightening his grip on the gun. "Don't be stupid enough to think you're faster than my finger is on the trigger. Drop whatever's in your hand."

The candle hit the floor with a thud. Jeremy saw that the two other men had guns trained on his terrified children.

"What do you want?" Jeremy asked.

"Just your food. Now give me your flashlight."

He handed it over. Slowly.

"Go stand over there." The gunman jerked his head toward Jo and the children.

"C'mon. You have to leave *something* for my kids." As dangerous as the situation was, Jeremy couldn't just let them walk out of the house with the last of the food. Crossing the room, he put himself between the shooters and his family. The kids huddled behind him, whimpering into the back of his jeans, hiding from the violent confrontation taking place in their living room.

"Got kids of my own, mister."

Outside, past the open door, a hellish snowstorm of biblical strength howled through the night. Bursts of frigid air poured inside, reducing the temperature with startling swiftness.

The two other men retreated and searched the house. Jeremy could hear them going through closets and drawers, looking for a hidden stash. They hit the kitchen last, shoving food into backpacks.

Incensed, Jeremy could only stand there and watch.

"They didn't have very much," one of the men complained.

"Better than nothing." The lead shooter, gun and flashlight trained straight on Jeremy, backed out after his companions. The men covered their heads and faces and disappeared into the monster storm.

The second they were gone, Jeremy rushed over to slam the door shut. Broken, the locks rattled in their fittings.

The room was pitch black.

"Oh my God," Jo said. She sounded panicked. Shocked.

Shaken by the event, Jeremy nevertheless kept his cool in front of the kids. He pulled the second flashlight from his pocket, turned it on, and met Jo's eyes. "They're gone. It's okay. Grab a few towels and a chair from the kitchen?" He offered her the flashlight.

Jo, understanding his intent, took the flashlight. She went into the kitchen, leaving them in the dark, and then came back with a box of matches to light the candle Jeremy had dropped on the floor. That done, she headed upstairs.

"They had g...guns, Daddy," Lila whispered. She started crying. Little wrenching sobs that tore at Jeremy's heart.

"Shh. It'll be okay, baby." He crouched down and swept her up against his chest. Andrew and Haley latched on, clinging like barnacles to his arms.

"They took all our food."

"I know. They're as hungry as we are and they didn't know I would have shared if they'd just asked me to." He felt a perverse desire to lessen the threat of the intruders somehow, to make the experience less traumatic. Even if it meant lying about the food.

"I wouldn't have shared," Andrew said with shaky defiance. Candlelight reflected in his eyes. Jeremy understood the false bravado and squeezed his son tight.

Lila leaned her head back and fixed him with a round-eyed stare. Pixie-faced, dark hair in a girlish bob, she was the epitome of innocence. She said, "But what are we gonna eat?"

"Don't you worry about it, pumpkin. Daddy'll figure it out in the morning." He kissed her brow.

"I rechecked all the windows and braced the door to the garage," Jo said when she returned. She had an armful of towels, another flashlight, and a chair dragging behind her.

"Good. Why don't you take the kids upstairs, get them settled and ready for bed?"

"Aren't you coming up?" Jo asked, strain evident in her voice.

"In a little while." After being married for fifteen years, Jo was able to read the glance he sent her over the kids' heads: *I won't be sleeping tonight.*

Understanding, she nodded and herded the kids up the stairs.

When they were out of sight, he pressed his hands against his face and took a deep breath.

Jesus.

He spent the next five minutes stuffing towels into the shredded crevice between the frame and the door. Turning the chair around, he butted the back up under the loose knob and braced it. At least it would give him warning if anyone else tried to break in.

Making a quick trip upstairs, he collected the pistol and extra rounds of ammunition. In the office, he set the weapon on the desk next to the shortwave. Hovering over the radio, he twisted the knob slowly, searching for a clear signal. Praying for news. Waiting to hear that the cavalry had arrived with a shipment of food.

All he got was static.

In the morning, after an entire night of nervous pacing, Jeremy prepared to leave the house. When the snow first became an obstacle instead of a novelty, he and his neighbor Ed had fashioned makeshift snowshoes out of old tennis rackets. He strapped a pair onto his boots, tucked the gun into the deep pocket of his jacket, and put on the safety glasses he used for woodworking. It might have looked ridiculous, but it kept the stinging sleet out of his eyes. Grabbing a coil of rope, he waited for Jo to come down before he stepped out onto the porch. He wanted to make sure she braced the door after he left.

After tying the rope around a support column, he tied the other end around his wrist and gave it an experimental tug. Satisfied, he grabbed a shovel where it leaned against the wall and started down the walkway.

Like most of his neighbors, he cleared the path daily so they had access in and out of their house. Veering right, he used the shovel to help him climb the six foot drift in his front yard. Even when he crested the top and panned to look across the street, he had trouble seeing the houses. The landscape looked foreign, snow in every direction, the majestic homesteads seeming to sag under the weight of their white burden. It felt like being enclosed in a snow globe, like a bubble of perpetual fog and wind-whipped flurries cut them off from the rest of the world.

It was the most disorienting, freaky thing he'd ever experienced.

As an employee of Anaheim Hills, Jeremy had access to trucks outfitted with plows usually used for mudslides on highways. One sat at the curb. He'd used it every day back when the snow was still manageable; now it was a barely discernible lump, as useless as all the other vehicles.

He grunted and trudged on, tugging the rope every few feet to make sure he was still tethered to his house. Arriving at Ed's porch after what seemed like an hour, he unhooked the rope, set down the shovel and raised a hand to knock.

The ex-marine opened the door with a startling yank and a grim smile. "They get your food, too?"

Jeremy lowered his hand. He noticed a lump on Ed's forehead. "Yes. All of it."

"Come on in out of the cold." Ed, twenty years his senior and in fighting good shape, didn't appear bothered by his injury.

Jeremy undid the straps on the snowshoes and stepped inside. "Thanks. How do you think they were able to move through the storm like that?"

Ed closed the door. "Well, they knew the neighborhood. Probably used markers to find their way. Louise is sleeping," he said, explaining her absence. "She didn't get much after the bastards came in."

"They didn't hurt her, did they?"

"No, she's fine. Everyone all right at your house?"

"Yeah. I came over hoping you and Louise might have something to spare," Jeremy admitted. He hated the position he was in, but these were desperate times and men did desperate things to feed their hungry children. He paced a circle in Ed's living room.

"They even found my stash, or I'd split what was left," Ed said, sitting on the arm of the sofa.

"I know." Jeremy gave Ed a tight smile. "I couldn't raise any news reports on the shortwave last night. Not one report of supplies or deliveries. Nothing."

"Don't think we're gonna see any relief, Jer. They can't fly in with the weather like this and even if the National Guard is deployed, they're probably overwhelmed. I mean, imagine it. Every city, every state. We need to make a plan."

"What kind of a plan? We shared all our food with the neighbors back in the first few weeks. They might have a couple things left—if those thugs didn't get to them—but who's going to be willing to give up food when the rations are low and they have their own families to feed?" Jeremy experienced a pang of desperation unlike anything he'd felt before.

"I say we canvas the neighborhood anyway and see what

we turn up. Someone might have been holding out and will be willing to give you something if they hear your kids are hungry."

"All right. Let's go." Jeremy deferred to Ed's wisdom and expertise. The longer they stood there talking about it, the longer it would take to get the food home.

Ed rose and clapped a sturdy hand to his shoulder.

In less than ten minutes, they were outfitted for the weather, snowshoes strapped on, heads bent away from the wind. They carried shovels in case they needed to dig their way to someone's door. Using a buddy system, they tied themselves to each end of Ed's rope and followed the trees along the parkway.

The first three houses yielded nothing. The Reynolds, Bernard, and Diaz pantries were down to their last few jars of this or that, and they all had children that needed to eat. Jeremy discussed options, situations and plans, and then he and Ed moved on.

The snow blew sideways, relentless.

Rahn Ferrell, an accountant Jeremy had known for six years, opened his door, but only a few inches. The swarthy man darted wary looks between them that made Jeremy immediately think he had something to hide. Honest and respectable, Rahn had proven himself to be a good friend; today he looked shifty and nervous.

"Hey, Rahn. How are you and Candace doing?" Jeremy asked.

"She's ill and sleeping. What do you want?"

Taken aback by Rahn's abruptness, he said, "Were you hit by those thugs last night? They took all our food and I was wondering if you had something—anything—that I could give to my kids."

"We have nothing for you, Jeremy. Try Helen and Robert."

Through the crack in the door, Jeremy caught scent of a sickening stench. "We're on our way there next. Do you want us to—"

"Just go." Rahn closed the door and engaged the dead bolt with a solid snap.

Ed hooked Jeremy's elbow and drew him away from the Ferrell house.

"What the hell was that about?" Jeremy asked, dumbfounded. He adjusted the goggles over his eyes, shouting against the wind and sleet.

"I bet he killed Candace so the food would last longer. Probably toss her body out into the snow when it decomposes to the point he can't take the smell," Ed replied matter-of-factly.

Jeremy stopped dead at the end of the walkway and stared at Ed. "*Rahn?* Mild mannered, nice-as-pie Rahn? Never. He wouldn't do that to her."

Ed gave him a knowing, meaningful look. "People act differently when their lives are at stake."

Jeremy, disturbed at the thought, didn't say anything else about it.

Helen and Robert contributed two packets of oatmeal and a protein bar. The only bachelor on the street, Levin Black, gave Jeremy a can of peaches, eight pretzels and his best wishes. Although Levin smiled, there was something defeated in his eyes and posture, as if he was just waiting for the inevitable.

At the end of his own walkway, Jeremy tried to get Ed to take one of the packets of oatmeal and half the pretzels.

Ed glanced at the food with a contemplative look before accepting the packet of oatmeal. "Thanks, Jeremy. Let's get together tomorrow morning and decide what else we're going to do. Might have to make a trip to the store and see if there's anything left. We'll do what we have to."

We'll do what we have to. For some reason, the thought made Jeremy uneasy.

The meager meal had been met with squeals of excitement. While it lasted, Lila swooned over the peaches and Haley nibbled with relish at a pretzel and oatmeal. Andrew ate faster, wolfing his portion down, and complained his stomach was still rumbling when he was done.

That had been the night before. Now it was morning. Dressed once more to forage, Jeremy eyed his family with increasing distress. In the living room, Haley and Lila huddled together with their array of dolls, eyes luminous, mouths in little pouts. Jo sat on the couch, staring at the wall, a mug of hot water in her hand. They were out of coffee, out of hot chocolate, but the routine stayed the same. Andrew, usually rowdy and loud, sat subdued and silent in a pile of Lincoln Logs.

Jeremy's stomach growled constantly, grumbling and clenching with hunger pangs he forced himself to ignore.

"Come give me a kiss. I'm going to get us something else to eat." The kids brightened a little and ran over, peppering his cheeks with kisses. Jo glanced over, looking listless, but didn't get up.

Jeremy hugged the children hard against him until Haley squeaked in protest. After ensuring that Andrew would blockade the door with the chair, he left the house.

Outside, he bent to strap the snowshoes on and made sure the gun was in the pocket of his heavy coat. Getting his bearings, rope in hand, he started across the snow toward Ed's. He could only see a vague outline of the house through the swirling veil of white.

Cursing the weather under his breath, he slid down the

embankment to Ed's porch and brushed snow off his goggles.

The ex-marine swung the door open, already dressed and ready to go. Jeremy could see the days with so little food were starting to take a toll. Ed's face looked gaunt, eyes hollower than they were the day before.

"Where to first? Davidson's?" Jeremy asked. Located three blocks away, Davidson's was the biggest grocery store in town.

"Good enough place to start. We can hit the smaller stores afterward if we have to. Lot of times, they have vending machines in the employee lounges. I think we should tie ourselves together and move tree to tree along the parkway," Ed suggested, handing him a new length of rope.

"All right." Jeremy tied an end through his belt loop. Before the storm hit, he would have laughed at the thought of getting lost in a residential neighborhood.

After accepting one of the spare shovels, Jeremy took the lead. Twice he had to be redirected when he missed a tree altogether and started going in circles. They took three wrong turns, disoriented by the seemingly endless field of snow.

By the time Jeremy finally spotted the looming shape of the grocery store, two and a half hours had passed. Frustrated, exhausted and cold, he and Ed decided to go around to the loading dock in the back. Clearing the concrete steps with the shovels, they climbed up the platform and tried the door.

"It's unlocked," Jeremy said, twisting the knob. He went in, Ed on his heels.

The storage area they stepped into stretched along the entire back of the store. Jeremy glanced left and right, barely able to see in the gloom. Ed pulled a small flashlight from his pocket and pierced the darkness with a beam of light. He handed another flashlight to Jeremy.

"Doesn't look like there's anything but boxes back here. All the pallets look empty. Still, we should check them," Jeremy said, leaning the shovel against the wall. He clicked the flashlight on.

"I'll take the right, you take the left," Ed said. He propped his shovel against a pallet.

Jeremy wasted little time pawing through boxes and shelves, searching for even the smallest container of food. Sheets of plastic rustled when he shoved them aside to inspect a pile of crates. He found not one box of pasta, not one can of soup.

Nothing.

Meeting near the double swinging doors, he discovered that Ed hadn't turned up anything either.

Exchanging a grim glance, they pressed on.

Obviously ransacked several times, the supermarket had a chaotic appearance, shelves busted and tilting, shredded boxes littering the floor. Jeremy flipped the light switch at the back; to his surprise, the fluorescent bulbs overhead buzzed and flickered to life. The pale glow made the desperation around them more prominent, like a gritty photo from some post-apocalyptic world.

"Backup generator," Ed said, explaining the lights. "If we split up, we can cover more ground."

"All right. Shout if you run across anything." Jeremy banked left, finding useless plastic containers and random bits of trash. The frozen food section had nothing to offer except a discarded baggie and a rotting banana peel.

Jeremy marched up and down the aisles with increasing despair, pausing now and then to kick over a piece of flattened cardboard or lift a fallen shelf. He tucked the flashlight into his pocket to free his hands and make searching easier.

"Anything yet?" Ed called from somewhere else in the store.

"Nothing. You?"

"Not a damn thing," Ed said with disgust.

Jeremy cut his hips through a narrow half door into what was usually the fresh meat section. All the steel tables were clean and bare, as well as the freezer Jeremy found built into the wall. Coils of cold air spilled into the room while he stared at the empty shelves. He closed the door, leaning his forehead against the outside for a moment.

There were few places left to check. If there wasn't food here, there was little chance there would be food at the smaller convenience stores a few blocks down. The only other grocery store was miles from here, all but impossible to access.

He had a brief vision of turning into the kind of man who broke through someone's front door, gun in hand, demanding what was left of their food.

If there was any left at all.

Another vision, this one of Haley and Lila and Andrew's faces swam across his mind. Hungry faces, pleading eyes.

"I don't guess you found any food," a voice said behind him.

Jeremy whirled around, startled. A man stood there, layered in clothes and a thin coat, eyes haunted under the hood that covered his head.

"There's nothing left," Jeremy said, deciding on the truth. A strange tension hung in the air. Jeremy knew the other man felt it, too. He could see it in the man's dark eyes. Sense it in his posture.

"Haven't heard from anyone in weeks," the stranger said.

"Neither have we."

"We?"

"My wife and I," Jeremy clarified.

"So you live close by then?" The stranger rubbed his hand over his mouth in a calculating way Jeremy didn't like.

"Not too close. We have nothing anyway, if that's what you're wondering."

The man stared, cold and hard, as if trying to decide whether he was lying.

Jeremy said, "Why do you think I'm here?"

"You could have *something* though." The stranger raised his other hand; light glinted off a gun. "Tell me where you live."

Jeremy licked his lips. "There's hundreds of other houses you can check besides mine."

"I've checked quite a few. Lot of people are dead for one reason or another. And it's hard getting around, if you haven't noticed." He gestured with the gun. Impatient. "Tell me where you live."

An array of butcher knives in their holders sat to Jeremy's right, too far out of reach to be useful. In periphery, he saw Ed creep through the half door with a pipe raised. Although his eye was drawn there, Jeremy resisted the urge to glance.

"All right, man. All right," he said, showing his palms as signs of surrender. "I live on Juliet Drive. Twenty-four twenty-four."

With a mighty swing, Ed hit the stranger hard across the head. The man went straight down, landing with a heavy thump.

Jeremy hurried to retrieve the gun when it skittered across the floor. "He took me by surprise."

"Never even heard him come in," Ed said, staring at the man on the ground. A thick pool of red blood oozed toward the toes of his boots. Ed took a step back.

Jeremy frowned when he saw the blood and crouched close to feel for a pulse.

There wasn't one. He bowed his head in shock, bracing

the side of his wrist against his mouth. The gun hung limp from his fingers.

"Didn't mean to kill him," Ed said with a defensive edge to his voice. "But it's him or us."

"I know, I know. This whole thing is turning into an unbelievable nightmare." Jeremy stood up, glancing around like an answer to their problems might suddenly appear.

When he looked back at Ed, the older man was staring down at the prone body with a quizzical look.

"What is it?" Jeremy asked.

A brief look of disgust crossed Ed's face, and he tossed the pipe down. "You're not going to want to hear it."

Jeremy frowned. "What am I not going to want to hear? If you think you're going to jail for this, I'm not—"

"It's a shame to waste the meat." Ed met Jeremy's gaze dead on.

It took a moment for the insinuation to sink in.

"Oh *hell no*. Ed, you can't be serious." Jeremy turned away, yanking the beanie off his head. His stomach heaved at the very thought of...just *no*.

"Where are we going to get food?"

"Somewhere! If I have to go door to door for five miles in all directions, I will." Jeremy turned around and jabbed a finger at the dead stranger. "We're not resorting to that."

Ed continued to stare at him. Silent.

"I can't believe you're even suggesting it," Jeremy spat. "There's *no* way I'm feeding that to my kids."

"What will you do day after tomorrow, when they're crying and inconsolable because they're hungry? What will you do next week—"

"The storm will break by then. It has to. Relief is on the way." Agitated, Jeremy paced like a lion in a cage. Bile rose in the back of his throat.

"They can't relieve the whole country. We're in a world of hurt, son. You know it, and I know it."

"We can go up into the foothills. There's probably hundreds of rabbits—"

"In all this snow? We'll never find them. And even if we do, one little rabbit isn't going to feed a whole family. Much less two," Ed said.

"I *can't*."

"A man can do, and will do, anything he has to in order to feed his family." Ed turned the dead man over and started to remove his clothes.

"Ed..." Jeremy put a hand out in a clear *stop* gesture.

Ed didn't stop. He peeled the coat and layers of clothing off, tossing them unceremoniously aside. There was something eerily mechanical about his movements, as if even he didn't want to be doing what he was doing.

Jeremy paced faster. He set the gun on an empty counter and looked out into the ransacked store. The empty, teetering shelves mocked him. Through the high vents in the ceilings, around the cracks in the doors, he could hear the wind howling as the storm intensified.

Madness.

They couldn't be reduced to animals. There was another answer besides this. He heard one boot drop on the concrete floor. And then the other. Jeremy rubbed a hand down his face, taking several measured breaths.

His stomach rumbled.

No. *No.*

The sound of tearing paper turned Jeremy's attention back. Ed crouched down next to the stripped corpse on the cold floor and struggled to put a length of sterile paper half under the hip and thigh. A large butcher knife rested on the dead stranger's chest.

Jeremy looked away. Contemplated leaving the store altogether. If Ed wanted to take this road there was nothing he could do abou—

Chop. The thick, wet thud made Jeremy gag. He staggered into the main section of the store, curling his hand into a fist near his mouth. The end of a shelf caught his shoulder and he bounced off, stumbling over an overturned shopping cart. It made a ruckus, but Jeremy could still hear the steady chop of the butcher knife. Relentless.

Hacking the dead man into manageable pieces.

Jeremy threw up on the floor, hunched over with his hands braced against his knees. Hot, salty tears streamed from the corners of his eyes into the curve near his mouth and off his whiskered jaw. He shook with violent denial, both for what Ed was doing and for the crazy state of the world. Weeks of believing someone would eventually help them had led to this moment in time, where their very survival depended on making impossible choices that he didn't want to make.

He found the employee restroom and snapped on the light. It blinked and hissed like it might go out any second. At the sink, he turned on the faucet and rinsed his mouth of the foul taste. His stomach continued to rumble; he couldn't tell if it was in disgust or hunger.

Holding onto the edge of the counter, Jeremy Buckle tried to come to terms with his grisly situation. Going door to door had to be better than this. Someone out there had food. But he wasn't fool enough to believe strangers would give it up any easier than he would—Jeremy wasn't the only man with a family. He wasn't the only man suffering hunger pangs and fear.

By the time he left the bathroom, it felt like an hour had passed. Or maybe two or three. Jeremy couldn't be sure.

Ed stood outside the butcher's shop. A line of white wrapped packages sat atop the steel counter above the display case. As if this was just some other ordinary day and they were picking up meat for a barbecue.

It was so bizarre that Jeremy had to stop and orientate himself. He could see black writing across the paper: *Round steak. Flank steak. Rump roast.*

"Do the cooking yourself so the women don't ask questions about why it doesn't look *exactly* like the meat they're used to. If you use enough herbs and spices, it'll help disguise the taste," Ed said.

"How are you going to explain the blood on your clothes?" Jeremy asked, swallowing convulsively. He refused to think about eating human flesh.

"I'll tell Louise a shipment came in and I had to help do the butchering."

Shutting his mind down, Jeremy lurched forward and snatched several packages off the counter. He stuffed them into the pockets of his coat and a stray bag he found lying on the floor.

Jeremy said nothing as they gathered the dead man's remains and left.

With a shaking hand, Jeremy set a plate in front of each of the kids. Jo had hers on the table, utensils at the ready, salt and pepper shakers within reach. The children bubbled over with excitement and anticipation, forks held tight in their little fists, waiting for him to sit down. The house smelled ripe with fresh-cooked meat.

He sat at the head of the table, reluctant, avoiding the strange, questioning looks Jo gave him. He said a short prayer aloud and added a silent one for himself.

The kids dug in. They ate with gusto, chattering about how lucky Daddy was to get the last of a shipment of meat at the store. Jo kept trying to smile, too, apparently caught between relief and confusion.

Jeremy managed to smile before hanging his head and staring at his plate. After cooking it until the outside was almost black, he'd cut the "round steak" into bite-size pieces to help disguise it. He stared balefully at his portion. Because it was expected, he stabbed a piece with his fork and determinedly shoved it into his mouth.

It was hell to be starving and so repulsed at the same time. His stomach protested, and he dry heaved.

"Jeremy, what's the matter?" Jo asked.

"Nothing." The meat rolled around his mouth. He got up from the table and held up a finger to the rest of them. "Heard something outside. Be right back. Eat up."

Feeling like a traitor, like the biggest fraud ever born, he stepped outside and threw up. He threw up until bile painted the white snow a sickly yellow-green.

Jo opened the door and came out onto the porch. "Jeremy, what in the world is going on?"

"I think I caught a bug or something. Not feeling so great," he said, and it wasn't a lie. "I'll be in shortly."

She touched his shoulder, concerned, and went back inside.

Jeremy waited until the fit passed and retreated into his house.

Twelve days later when Ed appeared at his door, Jeremy said nothing. They exchanged a knowing look before Jeremy went to gather his makeshift snow shoes and coat.

Ed made pleasant small talk with Jo and the children, dropping hints that he thought there was a good chance another delivery had been made at the grocery store.

Inside, Jeremy cringed at the duplicity but methodically

laced up his boots and tucked the gun into the waistband of his jeans. He kissed Jo and the kids goodbye at the door.

"Bring back lots of meat again, Daddy!" Haley shouted.

Jeremy paled, then smiled. He wondered if the smile looked at all convincing. "You can count on it, sugar."

RESURRECTING EVE

J.A. Titus

"There, that should do it," the man said, a devilish smile creasing his face. He licked his lips and kissed the black box in his hands.

"Do you really think it'll work? I, uh, I mean, do you think we can bring her to life?" asked the second man.

Professor Arturo glanced slyly at his counterpart, Dr. Hurst, as he jammed his thumb down on the box's red button. "Let's sure as hell hope so."

The two men, dressed in white lab coats, stood over the assembled body parts on the table before them. Intricately stitched together, the nearly perfect pieces had been connected vein by vein and muscle by muscle.

"I feel like Dr. Frankenstein," Arturo said and laughed.

Hurst stepped back from his partner's side as the various machines and wires surrounding the table pulsed and sparked. The buzzing electricity and whistling sounds of the blood transfuser made him nervous, uneasy, but Hurst knew this had to be done. For the continuation of mankind, this had to work.

If their technique worked, the body on the table, this desperate experiment, would be the perfect woman. And, more importantly, the only woman left on Earth.

They'd been full of questions throughout the process. What if they were able to do this, only to have their creation die instantly? Would she succumb to the virus, the disease—whatever it was—that had killed off all the women in the world? If she survived, would she be able to carry a genetically altered fetus to full term? Would their efforts be futile? Were they wasting their time?

"Watch!" Arturo demanded.

"I can't!" Hurst exclaimed as he shielded his eyes from the blinding light surging through the room.

"Watch!"

Hurst opened his eyes and stared, wide-eyed with terror and wonder.

Did the body just twitch? Did it move?

Arturo jumped and danced in place, almost giddy as he cranked the large copper wheel beside the table. The electrical currents pulsed faster and stronger through the surrounding machinery. Hurst cupped his ears, afraid the vibrations would deafen him. The static buzzed around them, frizzing Arturo's neatly coifed hair. Hurst felt prickly hair on the back of his neck.

"It's a good thing I'm bald!" he cried out, his voice lost against the noise that penetrated the room.

"What?" Arturo responded, distractedly cupping a hand around one of his ears.

"I said it's a good thing I'm going bald!" Hurst yelled, this time even louder than before.

"What?"

Hurst frowned and shook his head at his partner. "Never mind."

Arturo shrugged and turned his attention back to the table.

The body on the slab twitched and convulsed with each electric surge. Her beautiful, creamy white eyes fluttered. Her right hand clenched and then relaxed, and the two scientists watched in silence, feverishly hoping their hard work would come to fruition. Arturo checked the Simbulas machine, tapped the meter and gave Hurst a quick wink.

"It's time," he mouthed.

Hurst flipped the large metal switch back, turning off the Simbulas machine and the electrical currents bombarding the body. The men stepped toward the table and watched, eagle-eyed, for any small movement.

Arturo licked his palm, taming his hair back into its familiar slicked-back style. "Give it time, Hurst," he said when his partner started drumming his fingers on the leg of his pants. He checked his watch.

"I don't think—" But before he could form another word, the patchwork body moaned.

Arturo stepped away from the table, his mouth agape. Another moan sounded, and the face, the one flawless, unstitched body part, scrunched up, puckering its lips as if it had tasted a lemon.

"By Jove, I think we've done it!" the professor squealed. He rushed back toward the slab and kneeled beside it. "Hello?" he whispered to the woman on the table.

Hurst stood back, unsure of what was happening.

"Westin," he said, dropping any pretense of formality. "Something's wrong."

Arturo waved his hands toward the doctor, keeping his eyes on the body. "Shh...shhh!" he urged.

Hurst stepped toward the door. He didn't feel right. He needed air, fresh air. "I think I need to step outside for a moment," he whispered.

The professor turned and saw Hurst across the room. "Where are you going? You're going to miss it." Turning back to the body, he stared, hands on the table but not quite touching the flesh. "Besides, have you forgotten what it's like out there?"

Hurst shuddered. He hadn't forgotten. With the fairer sex gone, many men had formed gangs, violent and intent on destruction. Everything was fair game, nothing was sacred. It was rare that an hour went by without a thundering boom or screaming air-horn sounding outside their underground laboratory. Men were turning into the savages women had long accused them of being. Before long, the idiots would all blow one another to Hell and the extinction of the human race would be complete.

A large number of the less aggressive men hid in makeshift underground shelters, scared to come out, afraid of getting their heads blown off. A few lucky ones had found old bomb shelters and claimed them. Arturo and Hurst had heard some of their ham-radio chatter, had even talked back on occasion.

Above ground, every street looked like something ripped out of a Bosnian history book. Smoldering buildings crumbled to the ground along the once-vibrant streets. Piles of rubble littered every corner, some of them only half-covering corpses no one had bothered to bury. The street signs were spray painted black, covered in angry red gang symbols. Once-prized vehicles were now scattered about, stripped down to bare metal carcasses, empty shells lying silent and immobile in the dangerous, lonely streets. All in all, the city looked like the war zone it was.

Long gone were the professional men who went to work every day to provide for their families, the decent, clean, dutiful men who strived to succeed. But maybe, just maybe, Professor Arturo and Dr. Hurst could turn everything around. It all depended on their piecemeal woman. If they could bring her back to life, perhaps they could also re-animate additional women. Maybe they would be able to end all this carnage and turmoil.

Another moan from the woman on the slab broke Hurst's train of thought. He wanted to feel hope, but what he felt instead was unease, guilt. He wasn't sure why, but he couldn't shake the feelings.

"Should we pump some more blood into her? Perhaps she's too weak to move again," he suggested.

"Yes, yes, that's an excellent idea!" Arturo, still kneeling, clapped his hands. "Why didn't I think of that?"

He jumped up and opened the door of a small refrigerator next to the Simbulas machine. The fridge contained dozens of bags of blood. Donor blood. O-. The professor pulled a bag out and attached it to the blood infuser.

"It's awfully quiet this evening," Hurst said. He hadn't heard an explosion for at least an hour.

"Maybe they blew themselves all up and we're the last men on earth."

Hurst scrunched his nose. "Wouldn't that defeat our purpose?"

Arturo moved closer, gave Hurst a quick kiss on the lips, and said, "I guess so."

Hurst took his hand, and they smiled at each other.

The humming from the blood pumping machine continued through the silence. The two men watched anxiously, their eyes glued to the body in front of them. Slowly, they began to see a change in the lifeless flesh. At first it was a small, almost minuscule difference in color, but then it began to grow, not stopping until the entire body became flushed with pink. It was a healthy color—the color of life.

The woman on the table spoke.

"I—" she said, her first word spoken through chapped, pink lips. "Where am I?"

The men's jaws dropped, but they said nothing. They had brought a dead woman, a piecemeal corpse, back to life. It had actually worked.

"Get the...video camera," Arturo said, his hands fluttering about as he tried to take in what had just happened.

Hurst tried to move, but he felt as if his feet were cemented to the tile floor. Trying to lift his legs felt like trying to lift fifty-pound burlap sacks filled with wet sand. "I'm stuck," he said, his voice barely more than a whisper.

"Quickly, man, quickly!" Arturo pleaded and turned toward his partner.

Hurst snapped out of the trance and grabbed the video camera bag from the counter beside the fridge full of blood. As he unzipped the bag, he kept his head turned toward the woman, not wanting to miss anything.

"Can you hear me?" Arturo asked her, speaking slowly, carefully.

The woman turned her head and faced him. She opened her eyes with a gasp. "Who are you? Where am I?" She tried to move, fear and frustration clearly visible in her expression when her body wouldn't respond. "What have you done to me? Where am I?" she asked, her voice high and shrilly now.

Hurst finally managed to pull the camera out and flip open the display screen. The camera beeped three times when he turned it on, drawing the woman's attention.

"Who is that? What do you want from me?" She twisted her head in Hurst's direction. The heart monitor beeped an ear-piercing alarm. Her heart rate soared well above the normal levels. Hurst cried out a warning, holding the video camera and zooming in on the monitor's screen, which now displayed 258 beats per minute.

"Westin, you'd better give her something or she's going to go into afib," he said. If the woman went into atrial fibrillation, she could easily throw a blood clot or have a stroke, and all their hard work would have been for nothing.

Arturo grabbed a syringe. Before his patient could ask what he was doing to her, he stabbed the needle into her chest and jammed his thumb down on the depressor, releasing the medication.

"Oh..." Her voice faded as the drug took effect.

Knowing it might cause her to panic, the doctor filled another syringe with Xanax. As he injected the calming drug into her IV, her head slumped to the side and her eyes fluttered closed. Within seconds, her heart rate had steadied and a quiet calm had returned to the lab. Arturo and Hurst stared first at the woman on the table and then at each other. They were both afraid to move or speak, not wanting to disrupt the peace.

"Keep filming," Arturo finally said.

Hurst raised the forgotten camera.

"My name is Professor Westin Arturo," he said, "and my handsome cameraman is Dr. Conrad Hurst." He walked around the slab and checked the bag of blood. It was empty.

Where is all the blood going? Hurst wondered.

As he moved to the fridge to grab another bag, Arturo put his hand on the patient's shoulder.

"Do you know your name?" he asked.

The machines all around the woman's body beeped and buzzed, but she did not respond. Arturo eyed Hurst. "Did you give her too much Xanax?"

Hurst responded with a scowl and shook his head.

Arturo returned the scowl with a frown and pressed a finger to his lips. "If you don't have a name and don't mind, I'd like to call you Shelley. Is that okay?" he asked the woman.

She replied with a soft moan.

"I think you gave her too much Xanax. I might have to flush her system if she doesn't get moving soon." Arturo prepared the second bag of blood and again pressed his forefinger to his lips, facing his partner across the woman's body. "Shelley is a lovely name. My favorite author's last name was Shelley," he continued. This time, the woman didn't respond at all.

The professor replaced the empty bag of blood with the

fresh one and stood beside the slab, watching as the new bag started to shrink. The blood was definitely flowing out rapidly, but where was it all going? He eased his hand under the woman's back, feeling for a puddle. Not finding one, he gently lifted the delicately stitched legs one by one to see if the blood might be pooling there. Nothing. The once cold limbs were now feverishly warm, and her skin maintained its healthy pink hue. He lifted her arm, traced the lines of blood vessels with his index finger, following along the map of arteries and veins as the blood continued to pulse through them. He traced his way from her wrist up her arm and on to her neck. As he reached her collarbone, the pulsing path split, the vessels going deep into her body and up her neck to her brain. He looked up at Hurst and motioned for him to come closer.

"The blood, I don't know where it's going," he whispered. His voice was shaky, and his Adam's apple bobbed up and down as he spoke.

Hurst handed the professor the video camera and pulled his stethoscope out from the pocket of his white lab coat. As Hurst listened to the woman's chest, Arturo zoomed the camera lens in on the veins in her neck, watching them throb as the infuser pumped blood through them. Hurst listened to the woman's stomach and jerked back.

"Her stomach is gurgling," he said. "Almost as if it's digesting." He pressed down harder and closed his eyes, trying to concentrate on what he was hearing.

"What in the world does this mean?" He pulled the stethoscope off and rubbed his temples.

"Shelley, can you hear me?" Arturo asked, panning the video camera from her toes to her forehead. He wanted to catch any movements she might make.

"Mm-hmm," she responded and twitched her leg.

"Shelley, do you think you could open your eyes?" the

professor asked, zooming the lens toward her face to catch the action.

"Mm-hmm," she replied again, and her eyes began to flutter open. Hurst kept a close watch on her movements, his back hunched and his brow furrowed as he paced beside the table. He wasn't quite sure what was going to happen, and he certainly wasn't sure about the rapid blood use.

"She needs more blood," Hurst said.

Arturo pointed the video camera toward the infuser and the nearly empty second bag of blood. "Remarkable!"

He took the video camera to the fridge and grabbed another bag. As he hooked it up, he said, "What do we do if we run out of blood?"

"How much do we have left?"

Arturo walked back to the fridge and opened the door. "Looks like about—"

"Shhh," Hurst said.

Arturo looked back, and the woman wiggled her foot.

"Up," she croaked. She jerked her right arm up awkwardly and let it drop off the side of the slab.

Arturo smiled, but Hurst met his toothy grin with a frown.

"We don't know what she's capable of," Hurst warned. "We need to be careful, follow protocol."

The professor cocked his head and shot Hurst an exasperated look. "Protocol? There's no protocol for something like this. And what do you mean *capable of*? What do you really think she could do? She's got to be reconditioned, retaught to use her muscles, to build up her strength, you know? What could she possibly do? She's only been alive a few minutes. She's like a baby."

Hurst sighed. He knew Arturo had a point. Shelley hadn't used the muscles of this new body before, and surely couldn't be capable of anything dangerous. His fatigue and worry were getting to him. "Okay," he conceded. "How do you want to do this?"

Once again, Arturo smiled. "She said she wanted to get up, right? Let's help her up."

"Do you want me to set up the tripod and record this?" Hurst asked.

"Of course, man, set it up." The professor moved around the slab, handed the video camera to his partner, and started unbuckling the straps holding Shelley down. While Hurst pulled out their tripod from the storage closet next to the laboratory exit, Arturo whispered in Shelley's ear: "We'll have you up in no time. Up on your feet! Isn't that wonderful?" He was so caught up in his own joy, he couldn't make out her mumbled response.

Hurst set up the tripod a few paces away from the table. He mounted the video camera and punched the record button. Moving back toward the table, he rolled up the sleeves of his white lab coat.

The doctor's movements exposed the sleeves of his old grey sweater. The professor eyed his partner carefully. He rested his hand on the table for balance. "You might want to roll down your sleeves," he said as he unfastened the last strap, this one holding Shelley's right leg down.

Hurst looked at his arms, narrowed his eyes, and pursed his lips. "And why is that, exactly?"

"You might get blood on your sweater if you don't. You don't want to get blood on your sweater."

Hurst walked to the opposite side of the table and pulled a reflex hammer from the pocket of his lab coat. "It's just an old sweater." He gently tapped the rubber tip of the hammer along Shelley's ankle, starting just below the stitching that held her foot onto her leg. He moved up along her right calf.

"It may be just an old sweater," Arturo replied, "but your mother gave it to you." He stood back and watched as Hurst moved along Shelley's limbs, testing them carefully and nodding with approval as she twitched.

"My mother's dead, Westin. She's not going to care if this sweater gets soiled."

The professor blustered.

Satisfied with the results of his reflex test, Hurst pulled a small flashlight out from his other pocket and stepped toward Shelley's head.

"Now, Shelley, I'm just going to check your sight. Are you able to open your eyes for me again?"

"Mm-hmm," she replied, her voice listless.

Hurst watched as her eyes fluttered. "Excellent. I just want to see if your pupils respond as expected, okay?"

Shelley responded with another *mm-hmm* and continued to stare, unblinking.

"But, Conrad," the professor continued, "that sweater is from Barneys of New York. Barneys! Do you really want blood and God knows whatever else all over an expensive, irreplaceable, sweater like that?"

Hurst sighed, biting back a response. After so many years together, he knew how unrelenting Arturo could be when it came to couture. He flashed the light around Shelley's eyes, delighted to see her pupils dilate and respond appropriately. Straightening, not wanting to risk a fight, he rolled down his sleeves.

Arturo smiled, rather smugly, and slid his left hand under Shelley's back.

"Let's lift her."

Hurst slid his own hand under her right side, and they each grabbed a limp hand.

"On the count of three," he said. "One...two...three!"

She sat up more easily than they'd expected and kept bending forward. Her forehead slammed into the metal table between her open legs.

Cursing and apologizing, they pulled her back into a sitting position.

Hurst shot Arturo an agitated glance. "Are you okay, Shelley? Did that hurt at all?"

No response.

"Perhaps we didn't reattach any nerve endings for the head?" the professor suggested. A lump formed on Shelley's forehead and swelled. "She doesn't seem to be in any pain."

Hurst shrugged. "I want to check her blood pressure. Can you hold her? And don't let her fall again. We want to avoid brain damage if we can."

Arturo obliged, clenching his jaw.

Hurst pulled the blood pressure cuff off a hook by the Simbulas machine. He slipped the cuff over Shelley's limp arm and put his stethoscope back on. His brow furrowed with concentration as he listened to Shelley's pulse. Her rapid heartbeat thundered in his ears, sounding like a speeding racehorse. He released the air from the cuff and frowned as the hand on the pressure gauge spun. "180 over 110," he whispered.

"What?"

"I said her blood pressure is 180 over 110."

"Isn't that bad?" the professor asked, concern in his voice.

Hurst shrugged, removed the cuff, and tucked his stethoscope back into his coat pocket. "I don't know if it's bad for her, but it's definitely bad for someone like you or me."

Arturo frowned.

"Shelley? Shelley, can you hear me?" Hurst asked, placing his palm on the small of her back and leaning closer to her perfectly stitched ears.

"I hear you," she croaked. Her voice was hoarse, muffled, like sound through a thin wall.

"How are you feeling right now? Does anything hurt? Are

you feeling any pain?" As he talked, Hurst grabbed his otoscope and looked for any leaking fluids in her ear. There were none. He removed the scope and watched as her head swayed.

"No. No pain," she finally replied.

"Are you feeling anything at all?" he asked.

She twisted her head to the side and gave him a lopsided smile. "I'm hungry. So hungr—"

"Hungry?" the professor interrupted. "You're hungry! Conrad, get our friend here some food."

"But—"

"No buts. Get her something to eat."

"Westin, I don't think that's—"

"Go!"

"Fine!" Hurst threw the otoscope onto the table beside Shelley and stomped off toward the kitchen. Before he shoved the door open, he looked back to see his partner leaning close and whispering something to Shelley. Some emotion that felt almost like jealousy surged through him. He kept his gaze on the pair of them for another moment. She looked odd, but he couldn't pinpoint why, exactly (aside from the Frankensteinian scars, of course). She sat there on the cold, hard slab, naked, her pieced-together body completely hairless, shaved and re-shaved during the many surgeries they'd performed, bald-headed, eyebrow-less. Her legs were sprawled open in front of her, and her arms hung by her sides. With her back hunched and her shoulders slouched, she reminded him of a depressed teenager. The professor continued whispering despite her unresponsiveness, but she just sat there like a life-size doll. Arturo wrapped his arms around her shoulders.

"Westin, I really...I think we should wait."

Arturo didn't respond other than to point toward the kitchen door. He continued whispering to the woman in his arms.

"Westin?"

"Just get the damned girl some food!" the professor bellowed and twisted around with a look of impatience.

Hurst sighed and pushed the laboratory door open. Fine! He'd get her some food, but he didn't have any idea how they were going to feed it to her. She could barely move her jaw to speak, let alone chew solid food. He stomped down the long, dark hallway toward their kitchen and tried to figure out what food could possibly be appropriate to feed her. They hadn't counted on her being hungry.

"Milkshake?" he muttered to himself and dismissed the idea. There was no way she'd be able to suck on a straw. He flipped on the light and stepped into the kitchen. The dead quiet of the room—a space in the unfinished part of the basement they'd repurposed after the world went to hell—had always disturbed him. He pawed through their stockpiled food, pulled out a can of chili, read the ingredients on the back, and shook his head when he saw the high fat content. She'd need more protein and plenty of carbohydrates to build her strength and muscles. He closed the cabinet door and headed toward the old tan ice box in the corner. It dated back to the late '40s or early '50s, the early years of his parents' marriage. He and Westin had had it restored when they remodeled their kitchen a few years back, and it had continued to run right through Armageddon. He pulled the door open, bent down, and peered at their meager provisions.

Spaghetti?

No. Too acidic.

Tuna fish?

Blech!

Leftover beef stew?

Hmm...that had potential.

He pulled out the small container, lifted the lid, gave the contents a quick sniff, and stuffed the leftovers into the microwave. While he waited for the stew to warm, he grabbed a spoon from the cutlery drawer.

The microwave dinged, and he pulled out the steaming bowl.

This will just have to do, whether Westin likes it or not, he thought as he flipped off the light switch. *I doubt she'll even be able to eat it. She needs a feeding tube before she tries solid food, but what Westin wants, Westin gets.*

He hurried back down the dark hallway. As he approached the laboratory door, he heard an odd sound. He paused for a moment.

Was that a thud? Is he trying to lift her up by himself?

Preparing himself for an argument, he squared his shoulders and kicked open the laboratory door. Nothing could have prepared him for what he found. Hurst's hands opened, and the plastic bowl of stew hit the floor, splattering his shoes and pants. His mouth opened, but no sound emerged.

There on the floor beside the table, legs folded beneath her and arms hanging at her sides, sat Shelley. A glistening red stain covered her face and chest. Thick blood dripped down her chin. She raised her head and looked at him. In front of Shelley's knees lay Westin, or what was left of him. His head, fully detached from his neck, sat on the floor beside her hip. His eyes bulged from his skull, hung like rotten grapes on his cheeks. His mouth formed a wide O, and blood ran out of his ears. Little pink bits of what appeared to be brain matter seeped from the top of his cracked skull.

The doctor buckled, gagging on the bile that filled his mouth, trying to un-smell the thick stink of blood, urine, and human waste. Shelley bent over Westin's neck stump and took a fierce bite of flesh. The sound of sinew snapping echoed through the otherwise quiet room. As she chewed the wet meat, Shelley looked up again. Her eyes narrowed to slits. Blood poured from her mouth as she fed.

Too shocked for words, Hurst just stood there and watched as the monster they had created dug into his partner's chest cavity like an animal, her once weak jaws finding new strength with each bloody, flesh-filled bite. He felt an instinctive need to run, to get away, but his feet were stuck to the floor. Seconds that felt like an eternity passed before he was finally able to raise his shaking hands to his face. He hid his eyes behind them, but the sound of the reanimated monstrosity devouring the professor continued to torment him. That beast was eating his partner, his lover, his everything. He fell to his knees with a hard thud. His kneecaps smacked against the concrete.

Open your eyes, he thought.

He tried and couldn't.

The munching and crunching sounds finally stopped, and the room fell silent for a brief moment.

Something shuffled toward him.

He jumped and gave a little scream when a burst of hot breath wafted against his bald head and the sound of panting moved right in front of his face.

He waited for the attack. When it didn't come, he lifted his eyes and looked up. Shelley, covered in blood, stared down at him. Her lips curled into a genuine smile, then parted to reveal her horribly sharp teeth.

She sat down in front of him, returning his gaze with curiosity. Her breathing slowed to a normal pace. With jerky movements, she lifted her right hand to wipe the blood from her face. With an almost cat-like motion, she then proceeded to lick the hand clean. She met his eyes, stopped, and smiled again.

"I'm not hungry anymore," she purred.

NAROBRIAN AFTERNOON

ROBIN MORRIS

The phone rang as Lori carried the basket of laundry in from the garage, stepping carefully because she couldn't see if Zane and Greg were underfoot. At the same time the dog started barking, a rough, angry bark that was unusual for the part poodle, part who-knows-what mutt that they adopted just before moving out to the middle of nowhere.

She dropped the laundry basket onto the kitchen counter and reached for the phone, only to find the handset missing. Where had she put the thing? It was Steve who never put it back, but maybe she'd taken it into the garage like she sometimes did when she was expecting Steve to call. She wasn't expecting him to call, though, he'd left in the company van pool as usual that morning and would be back around six.

"Zaaaaaaaaaaane!" Greg shouted from somewhere, his toddler shriek drowning out the sound of the phone for a second. When he quieted down, she was able to follow the ringing to Steve's favorite living room chair.

"My dinosaur!" Zane shouted, sounding more like a tornado siren than a five-year-old boy.

Where were they?

She grabbed the phone, pressed the talk button, said "Hello," and turned to find the boys.

"Don't panic, honey," Steve said on the phone, "just get out of town."

"Miiiiiiine!" One of Greg's favorite words filled the house.

'"What?" she said. The dog barked, even louder.

"Get in the car, go to a motel," Steve said. "Are the kids all right?"

She stepped into the kitchen again. "Of course they're all right. They're playing with a toy dinosaur."

Toy dinosaur? she thought. *When did they get a toy dinosaur?*

"Lori that's not—" Steve shouted.

The phone went dead. Lori shook it. She tried to call Steve back, but there was no dial tone.

Annoyed, she found her cell phone in her purse. The phone's screen showed no bars and flashed NO SIGNAL. The tower in the center of town had an antenna that pulled down satellite TV and radio and served as the cell phone tower for the town as well as the only connection to the world. No one was allowed to have their own satellite TV or radios. That made Lori uncomfortable, but very few agreed with her because all these services were free.

Greg walked across the kitchen floor, his diaper dragging behind him, leaving a wet trail behind it. She rushed to him and put a hand on his shoulder. He pointed back at the door to the garage, which was open. "Mine," he said.

She was always careful to close that door. The garage wasn't safe with its short stairway and lawn tools hanging on the walls, not to mention the dryer that could seem like a cave to explore and the car the boys might think was a fort to crawl around on. The door was open now. Did she forget to close it when she raced to answer the phone?

The dog barked in the garage. Was Zane in there too?

"You're all wet, honey," she said to Greg. His diaper had reached the limit of its absorbent powers and fallen down to the two-year-old's feet, leaving him naked under his damp Sponge Bob shirt.

She picked him up, leaving the diaper on the floor. His shirt squished against hers. She wanted to check on Zane first. If he *was* in the garage, who knew what he might be doing in the there. Lori carried Greg through the garage door.

The garage was at least two feet deep in water. The pool came up to the tops of the wheels on the car and poured through the open dryer door.

Had a pipe burst?

No, she could smell salt. Sea water.

Fuffy continued to bark. "Fuffy" because Zane couldn't say "Fluffy" when they got the dog. Lori wished he would shut up.

Zane said, "Look Mommy I found a dinosaur." Then he screamed. He was on the stairs, knee deep in water. He held some wriggling *thing*. It was dark brown, maybe green, with little limbs, a squat head, and a snout full of teeth. Some kind of lizard, but not.

The thing had its mouth around Zane's arm. Blood dripped down to his elbow. Holding Greg tightly, she leaned over and smacked the creature as hard as she could.

The blow was hard enough to dislodge the lizard. When it dropped off Zane's arm, she caught it around the neck and pulled it away from him. Zane held out his bleeding arm and wailed.

The lizard thing was strong. It struggled in her grip, managed to pull out of her hand, and fell to the top step.

Fuffy barked, and Zane screeched. Lori suddenly needed a few dozen aspirin.

The lizard stood on two legs.

Lizards don't stand on two legs. No wonder Zane called it a dinosaur.

Whatever it was, it was another reason to get the hell out of this town.

The lizard turned and ran toward Lori. She kicked it. The toe of her sneaker caught the lizard under its snout and sent the creature sailing across the garage. It slammed into the far wall and fell down behind the washer and dryer.

"Come on," Lori said to Zane and took him by the hand. He stepped up out of the water, dripping all over the top step. Fuffy wouldn't stop barking. He stared into the watery garage.

"Shut up, Fuffy," Lori said. "It's gone." She pulled Zane into the house, into the brighter hallway where she could examine his arm. It wasn't too bad, just deep scratches. She would wrap it in something, then take him to the hospital. The company hospital of course, free to town residents.

Fuffy yelped. Lori glanced into the garage. Something huge—much bigger than the little lizard, something like a crocodile but uglier—slid back into the water with Fuffy's little tail sticking out between its jagged teeth. It disappeared without a splash.

Lori slammed the garage door and locked it. So much for the car. Even if the water hadn't flooded the car's engine, there was no way she was going back in there after it.

As she backed away from the garage door, water seeped beneath it and ran onto the kitchen floor.

She had to put Greg down so she could grab a kitchen towel and wrap it around Zane's arm. Greg made an anxious sound and raised his arms, wanting her to pick him up.

She thought about Steve's call, his warning. *Just get out of town*, he'd said. But what was happening? Where had the salt water come from, and what did Steve know about it? What the hell was happening out there? She heard more sloshing water under the house and another noise coming from outside. A splashing, pulsing sound. Almost like... waves. But that couldn't be, could it?

"I need you to be a big boy," she told Zane. He nodded,

his face serious, looking very much like his father. He sniffled a little but seemed to be under control. "We need to get some clothing together and leave the house. Put your favorite clothes in your backpack while I help Greg."

The house was a single story, one of three models offered to company families when they moved to town. All three models were cheap replicas of Spanish style houses, with tile roofs and fake adobe walls. Mortgages were paid as paycheck deductions. It was simple to get a mortgage in Collins: just be an employee of Collins Research Ltd. The company employed everyone in town.

Her feet squished on the wet carpet of the boys' room. Zane's bed was on one side and Greg's crib on the other. She clicked the light switch. Nothing happened. Burnt-out bulb or power outage? She guessed it didn't matter. There was enough light coming in through the windows to see by.

She put Greg on the changing table while Zane packed his little backpack. She quickly got Greg into a new diaper, pants and shoes, and a dry shirt, this one with Bob the Builder on it.

"Why do we have to go?" Zane asked. He had packed the stuffed panda he used as a pillow inside. She almost told him not to take it but decided the only thing she really cared about right then was getting out of the house.

A shadow filled the door. They turned toward it, and in a moment a creature appeared at the threshold. It was another lizard on two legs, but this one was five feet tall. It had a long neck and nasty looking claws on each foot that could probably disembowel a person with one stroke.

The thing stood there, seemingly trying to decide whether to go for the appetizers or the full meal. Lori picked a toy fire truck off the floor and threw it at the creature. Then she threw a Buzz Lightyear figure, a basket of diapers, and the baby monitor that still sat near the crib.

Getting into the spirit of things, Zane started throwing toys at the monster too. When it made an annoyed sound and backed off a step, Lori pushed the crib against the door, slamming it shut. "That's why we have to leave," she said. Then she upended Zane's bed and pushed that against the door as well.

"That was a real dinosaur, wasn't it?" Zane asked.

"Dinosaur!" Greg said, pronouncing the word surprisingly well.

"Dinosaurs are extinct," Lori said. She took Greg off the changing table and held him. He looked around, quite excited by what was going on.

"But Mom—"

"How are we going to get out of here?" she asked, not expecting an answer from the boys.

The window. It was the only way. She looked outside and finally saw the full extent of the unfolding disaster. Water splashed against the house, inches under the window. The view was water, water, and more water. The town was in the water, under the water. Only a few of the Spanish tile roofs showed above it. She had chosen the house on the edge of the valley because she liked the view. Or maybe just to be as far as possible from the tower in the center of town, the HQ of Collins Research Ltd. That put the house at a higher elevation than most of the homes.

Although she never could have known it at the time, she realized now that that choice had saved her life, and those of her children. She tried not to think about the others, the scientists and their wives, husbands, and children. It wasn't a flood, it was more like a *sea* into which someone had dropped a bunch of cheap houses.

And Steve? She could see the top of the tower. He'd told her his lab was deep underground, but maybe it wasn't flooded. She had to believe that.

• • •

She had a Ph.D. in history, and she had assumed she would be a professor, but universities weren't hiring. Steve had his own doctorate in an area of atomic physics so rarified that only ten people in the world could pronounce it. In another time, his expertise might have gotten him some deeply classified position within the government, but even top-secret budgets were on hold these days.

Then Collins Research came calling. You have to move to our location, they'd said. It's all very hush-hush. You have to sign a contract with terms that would make a lawyer's hair turn white.

It had been the only offer either of them had, so they packed up and drove from the east coast to a town that was still being built when they arrived.

He couldn't tell her about his work. That was absolute. The contract stipulated that anyone who told anything to anyone would be fired instantly, and the implication was that the blabber would never work in his or her chosen field again. Lori didn't like it, but Steve said, "Five years, then we'll have enough money to move wherever we want, and you can look for work in your field too."

She'd agreed. What else could she do?

All of that now seemed like it had happened a million years ago.

They had to get on the roof.

It might not buy them much time, but it was the only option she could think of.

But how? The roof stuck out above the window. Was there any way to grab it? What if she got in the water?

Could she reach up high enough to grab the gutter? Would the gutter hold?

She looked back at Zane. The water in the room was higher, up to his shins. They couldn't stay.

BANG! Something hit the door from outside. The crib and the bed shifted.

They *really* couldn't stay.

Lori put Greg back on the changing table and opened the window, glad it was a big one and not some small hole she'd have to force herself through. Strong wind brought the sharp scent of sea water into the room. She pushed the table against the window. Greg giggled as it moved.

BANG! The bed holding the door closed slid down a little.

"Where did the water come from?" Zane asked.

"I don't know." She attacked a shelving unit that had kids' clothing on it. She pulled a shelf free.

"Why is the water stinky?"

"It's salty. Don't drink it." She glanced back. Zane was knee deep. She put the shelf through the railing. It stuck out the window over the water like a diving board.

Would it hold?

"Are you making a fort?" Zane asked.

"We're going on the roof," she told Zane. "I'm putting Greg up there first, then I'll take you up with me." Lori placed the remaining shelves into the base of the changing table to help hold the table in place. She needed something to hold them down. She looked around.

BANG! The door cracked open, and the big reptile poked its snout in.

"Mommmmmmm," Zane said.

She dragged a low bookcase to the window, grunting with the effort, and pushed it face down on the shelves. It would have to do. She picked up Greg. Climbing up on the pile of furniture, she edged out onto the shelf. The shelf didn't immediately crack and dump her and Greg into the seawater. She grabbed the gutter and looked over it onto the roof. No dinosaurs.

Dinosaurs. Now even *she* was thinking like a child. They couldn't be dinosaurs.

It wasn't easy to get Greg up on the roof with one hand while holding the gutter with the other. She placed him on his rear on the Spanish tiles.

She would have to take her eyes off of Greg for thirty seconds or so while she helped Zane. She didn't want to do it, pictured Greg sliding off the roof and into the rising water, but she didn't have the strength to pull all three of them up at once. It was this or wait here in the bedroom for the creature to break through the door. At least the roof wasn't steep. At least she had *some* chance of making it work.

She looked down, into the bedroom. Zane looked at her with wide eyes, as if he'd just had a horrible thought.

"Is Fuffy going with us?" he asked.

The bedroom door banged open a little wider. Lori saw one scaly hand/paw/whatever enter the room. Next came a snout. The shelf bent under her weight.

"No, honey, he can't come. Now climb up here."

"Why can't Fuffy come?"

She sense one of his epic tantrums coming on. They started with sniffling and ended with a screaming fit.

"He's, uh, guarding the house," she said, trying to head it off.

"I WANT FUFFY!" Zane screamed. Behind him, the reptile thing clambered over the furniture that was no longer holding the door closed.

She jumped forward without thinking. That thing was not going to get her son.

"I WANT FUFFY I WANT FUFFY!"

She snatched Zane up as the reptile jumped. It landed right where Zane had just been. Lori turned and shuffled back out onto the bowed shelf. The thing snapped at her heels, lightning quick. Zane bawled in her ear, crying but no longer shouting.

One hand firmly around Zane, her other hand gripped the gutter. She put all her weight on that hand and lifted her feet. The reptile snapped at her rear, its teeth tearing her pants, but it had not noticed its precarious footing. It reached the end of the shelf and fell into the water below. It thrashed and bellowed loudly, then went under.

Lori put her feet back on the shelf.

"Fuffy," Zane whispered.

"Fuffy saved us," she told him.

"He did?"

She nodded. "When he barked I knew there was trouble."

"He's guarding the house?"

"That's right. Can you climb up?" She pushed on his rear until he was up on the roof. "Is Greg all right?"

There was no answer. She pulled herself up until she could see. At first she thought the things flying around the house were seagulls. Greg stood, high on the roof, raptly watching the birds. They swooped down, snapping their beaks. Long beaks, lined with teeth.

Zane stood nearby, looking scared. One of the birds landed on the roof and walked toward Greg. Then more landed. They were almost as tall as the two year old, and clearly considered him an afternoon snack.

Lori pulled herself onto the roof, or tried to. The section of gutter pulled away from the house and she landed back on the shelf.

"ZAAAAAAANE!" she yelled. "Stand next to Greg! Shout at the birds. Wave your arms. Try to scare them away!"

She launched herself at a different section of gutter that was still attached to the house. If it failed she would fall in the drink and her kids would be bird food. It held, and she swung her feet up onto the Spanish tile. It was a little awkward to push herself up, but in a moment she was on her feet, and running.

"Shoo! Go away!" she shouted as she ran toward her kids. Zane stood next to his brother. The large birds showed no fear of her at all. Lori kicked one and it fell away, squawking. She tried to guard the boys, moving around to cover all angles. When she turned one way the birds approached again from her rear. She had to turn around and around to make them flap their wings and move back.

"Go find a garbage dump! Filthy things!"

Finally the birds on the roof gave up and took to the air, but they didn't go very far. The flock wheeled around the roof, looking for an opening.

"Everyone all right?" she asked and looked around. For the first time she was aware of the sky. Low clouds made the day dark. It looked like rain, and a lot of it.

Lori kneeled and hugged the boys. "Good job, Zane," she said.

"Birdies!" Greg said, pointing up.

"I was scared, Mom." She felt Zane shivering against her as she held him close.

"Tell you a secret. So was I."

The roof was an island, but it wasn't far from shore. Waves lapped against the lip of the valley and the jungle beyond.

"I believe you now, Zane."

"Believe what?"

"They are real dinosaurs. Look that way. Don't be scared, it's far away."

Zane looked where she pointed. Some distance down the beach a Tyrannosaurus Rex, or one of its close relatives, tore chunks of flesh out of a corpse the size of three houses. It couldn't be anything else, certainly nothing that existed in the modern world.

Zane stiffened, and his eyes went wide.

"It's okay," Lori said. "It's eating. It doesn't care about us."

"Barney!" Greg said.

Lori grimaced. Greg had learned to run the DVD player soon after he started to walk. The purple menace's theme song was forever stuck in her head.

"I want to go home," Zane said.

"We're standing on top of it."

"I mean Boston."

"Oh. Me too." She was surprised he remembered it. Their tiny apartment in a questionable neighborhood seemed like heaven now.

Lori assessed the situation. It wasn't good. They had left the house without Zane's backpack, the diaper bag for Greg, her purse, or any means of communication. Usually going out with the kids meant carrying more gear than a hiker on the Appalachian Trail. She had nothing.

And they were standing on the roof of the house surrounded by water with killer birds overhead.

At least she had some time to think about what to do next; no more dinosaurs could get to them for now.

Unless they could swim.

She pushed that thought out of her head.

A flash of lightning filled the sky, and a moment later thunder rolled across the valley.

Don't let it rain.

It started to rain. Not too hard at first, but dark clouds in the distance promised a lot more.

"Mom," Zane said. "Mom. Mom."

She sat on the roof and pulled Zane into a hug. She wanted to tell him it was all right, but it wasn't.

"I'm thinking," she said. She sat Greg on her lap. She would protect them to her last breath, but she didn't know what to do.

Were all her neighbors dead? Drowned in their houses? The scientists would be in the tower, alive she hoped. But all the wives, and kids, and a few house husbands? What was happening? How could it happen? Grief and confusion threatened to overwhelm her, but she had to keep her head together for Zane and Greg.

She kicked at a bird that landed on the roof near them. It took off. Rain did a dance on her head, the water trickling down. All three of them were soaked.

The water level was completely up to the roof line now. The inside of the house would be filled.

Two fins moved by the house, then one submerged. She couldn't believe it.

Sharks? Did they have sharks in dinosaur times? Whatever they were, they circled behind the house and out of sight.

That ruined any idea of swimming to shore.

Greg raised his arms and made a bubbling noise with his lips. Zane leaned against her.

"Zane? Honey?" she wanted him to stand so she could move.

Zane was asleep. Eyes closed, completely out. Amazing. She didn't think she'd ever be able to sleep again.

Waves lapped up the roof, within about two feet of Lori's legs now. If this kept up, they would be swimming, like it or not. One of the fins surfaced. A huge, dark shadow moved through the water below.

The other fin moved in the opposite direction, past the house.

The sharks must have been licking their lips—or whatever the shark equivalent of lips was.

She touched Zane on the head to wake him up. "We have to move," she told him. She tried to stand up, first putting Greg on the roof next to her. Zane fell into her lap, still sleeping. As she scooted her butt higher on the roof, one of the sharks jumped out of the water and landed on the shingles. Its teeth snapped just an inch from Lori's foot.

She scooted backward fast, trying to bring both boys with her. She gripped them hard, jerked them toward safety.

The shark slid back down the slanted roof. Its toothy grin seemed to say, "Next time." The weight of the huge carnivorous fish, at least as big as the Great Whites she saw on Shark Week, tore away shingles and exposed the decking.

"Mommy, that hurts," Zane said. Greg started to cry.

At least Zane was awake. She loosened her grip on him.

"We need to stay alert, kids," she said. "We have kind of a situation here." The shark fins circled the house.

"Eeeeeeew," Zane said and put his hand over his nose. "Greg's stinky."

He was right. Greg's diaper was loaded. Her maternal instinct was to change him, but of course she couldn't. She managed to stand up and picked up Greg. He reeked.

"Come on," she told Zane. They moved up to the highest point on the roof.

"Why is the water higher?" Zane asked. "Why—" his eyes grew big. He saw the fins in the water. He watched Shark Week too.

"We're safe up here," Lori said. One of the fins cruised closer still. The rain intensified.

Her foot slid on the tiles. She almost dropped Greg. Some kind of pipe stuck up through the roof. It had a cap on it to keep rain out. Ventilation over the stove? Maybe. It didn't matter. It was something to hold on to.

"Grab onto this," she told Zane. He did, for once not asking why. Greg continued crying. She tried to comfort him, but it was hard. She needed someone to comfort her.

The roof shook, and her feet flew out from under her. She landed hard on her side, pain shooting up and down her body. She managed not to drop Greg, but that meant hitting an elbow on the hard tile, and that hurt a lot.

"Mommyyyyyy!" Zane shouted. He lay on the roof, clutching the pipe. Lori slid down the roof on her belly. Toward the water. And the sharks. She reached her free hand up and managed to grab the ridge of the roof, but her fingers slipped on the wet shingles, unable to find purchase.

She slid farther down, wanting to push Greg up, to save him at least, but knowing he'd have no more luck holding on than she'd had. This was it. The sharks would feed and this primordial world would win. She couldn't see the shark jump again, but she felt it thump against the roof. She kicked at the tiles, trying to slow herself, delay the inevitable. Zane stared down at her with wide, unblinking eyes.

She wished she could see Steve one last time.

A roaring, mechanical sound filled the air. Then it changed tone, and a warm liquid splashed against her. As she continued her slow slide, dark red liquid and gobs of meat landed in puddles all around her.

The roaring noise stopped. Lori's legs hit something that kept her from sliding into the water.

Lori flipped onto her back and tried to make sense of what she was seeing.

"You all right, girl," a voice said. "It's sushi."

"Mrs. Graden?"

"I told you call me Bonnie."

The woman had to be a hallucination. Lori blinked. She was in the afterlife, or she was dreaming. Bonnie Graden, grandmother of Kenny, the young star of the scientific staff at Collins Research Ltd., stood in a small boat bobbing up and down next to her demolished roof, holding a chainsaw.

Pieces of shark and shark blood lay everywhere. The shark's head, full of wickedly sharp teeth, bobbed in the water next to the boat. The rest of it was gone.

"Come on," Bonnie said. "Get you and your young ones in here." She put the chainsaw down and held out her hands.

Lori managed to stand, but the roof was even more slippery now than before, so she stepped very carefully. She handed Greg to Bonnie, who pulled him close to her. "Whoooie. This child needs changing," she said.

Lori scrambled back up the roof, scanning the surrounding waters for the second shark, trying hard to remember to breathe.

At first, Zane wouldn't let go of the pipe. He stared at Bonnie, trembling.

"It's all right," Lori said. "You know Mrs. Graden. The boat's safe."

When he loosened his grip, she picked him up.

Getting Zane and herself into the boat wasn't easy. He wouldn't let her hand him off to Bonnie, and the boat swayed erratically. But she did get in finally and sat on one of the wooden seats with Zane in her lap.

"Where did you find a boat?" she asked. It seemed like both a stupid question and the only question that really mattered.

"It was floating along, no one to claim it. Maybe that Mr. Feldman owned it, he always talks about fishing." She handed Greg back to Lori.

Lori didn't know Bonnie all that well, but everyone in town knew her story. She grew up in Watts, the African American community in Los Angeles. She had a daughter at sixteen, and the daughter had a son at seventeen. When her daughter died of an overdose, Bonnie was left caring for her grandson, Kenny.

Kenny turned out to be a science prodigy. He finished high school at twelve and college at fifteen. He was in grad school when Collins Research came calling. They paid through the nose to get him.

"Thank you so much," Lori said. "If you hadn't come along, we—"

"Just glad to find some folks alive," Bonnie said. "You don't know how many dead ones I seen." She sat at the back of the boat and turned to the outboard motor.

"You haven't found anyone else?"

"Nope. I figure we head to the tower, check on the men." She meant the scientists. There were a few women among the elite team Collins had assembled, including Helen Feldman, wife of the fisherman.

"Steve called just when it started," Lori said. "Then the phone went dead."

"Glad to here it. He say anything about Kenny?"

"No, I'm sorry."

Bonnie handed Greg back and turned to the motor. "Push us away," she said.

Lori leaned over and pushed against the bloody roof tiles with her foot. When the boat was clear, Bonnie started the engine and the boat moved away from the house.

"What's this?" Bonnie asked, pointing to the towel wrapped around Zane's arm.

"He was bitten by a—"

"Dinosaur," Bonnie finished. "What they have to be, right?"

"Yeah, but I can't explain it."

"I don't explain it, I just try to keep alive. I sliced up a few of them dinos with my friend here." She patted the chainsaw. "They was just suddenly in my house. But I, well, I kind of been ordering a lot of stuff on the computer. With Kenny making so much, I couldn't resist."

"You ordered a chainsaw online?"

She nodded. "Had a dead tree in the back yard needed taking care of. Wanted to do it myself. Ordered some other stuff would be useful now, but I couldn't get to it."

"I miss real shopping," Lori said. Everyone ordered everything online in Collins.

"Me too. Love that Home Depot." Bonnie steered the boat through the choppy waves toward the top stories of the Collins tower sticking up through the new ocean. The sky bloomed with lightning again. A clap of thunder followed, and the rain poured harder than ever.

A group of enormous birds floated on the water like ducks. They were skinnier than ducks, though, and at least five feet long from beak to tail. They had little stubby wings like chickens. They didn't look like they could fly, but their legs moved them through the water quite fast.

"Watch out," Lori said.

"These ones never attack," Bonnie said. One of the birds dived underwater and came up with a fish. It tilted its head back, and the fish slid down its throat.

"At least there's one thing that doesn't want to eat us," Lori said with relief.

The water under one of the birds erupted as something impossibly huge came up from underneath and swallowed the bird whole. The creature had a long snout with many teeth. It had whale-like flippers and a head the size of a car.

The thing sank back into the water, sending a wave in all directions. The boat rocked madly.

"What the hell?" Lori shouted. She held Greg in her arms, and Zane clutched her leg. Greg wailed.

"WHAT THE HELL?" she repeated.

Bonnie expressed herself with much stronger language.

"Make it go away, Mommy," Zane said.

The thing, the monster, must have seen them when it jumped. It came back, sliding under the boat. There was no fin on the top; it was no shark. First its head, then a long sinuous body went by.

The thing kept coming and coming. It was as long as a semi trailer truck, at least.

"I have never heard of anything like that."

"Kenny loved dinosaurs when he was little," Bonnie said. "His books talked about some mighty big ones lived in the water."

The creature dived, its tail still visible for a while until the whole animal disappeared into the depths. Bonnie sped up the motor. The front of the boat rose and fell, slapping the water and sending up spray.

"Look down, tell me if you see it," Bonnie said.

Lori looked. The water was dark and murky. Greg still cried loudly, and Zane clung to her.

"Turn left!" Lori shouted. Bonnie steered to the left, and the huge head of the creature missed when it came up. It snapped at air instead of cutting the boat in two. It fell back in the water, producing another series of enormous waves.

Lori frantically looked all around to see where the thing would come up again. It was very hard while holding Greg and with Zane clinging to her.

There was a moment when they thought they had left the creature behind. The motor strained. The tower in the center of town got closer.

Instead of breaching like a whale this time, the thing came a little out of the water ahead of the boat. Then it quickly dived. This threw up a large wave.

When the boat hit the wave, it almost completely left the water. Its nose sailed up, then down at an angle that took it into the water. Lori flew into the air. The back of the boat hit the water hard, sending a wall of water outward. Lori came down on the seat with a painful thump. She squeezed the boys harder than ever, and looked toward Bonnie, who had almost lost her grip on the motor control.

She felt Zane trembling with fear. Greg redoubled his crying.

Another wave hit the boat from another direction.

"It's trying to swamp us," Lori said.

The boat tilted from side to side.

"Maybe I can kill it with my little friend," Bonnie said. "Or at least wound it." She bent down.

"Where is it?"

Lori looked too. There was no chainsaw in the boat. It must have flown out when the boat went airborne.

"Zig zag," Lori said.

"What?"

"Drive side to side, fast." Lori moved her hand like a snake.

Bonnie pressed the motor control. "Damn," she muttered. She pulled the starter cord.

"Oh no," Lori said.

"I'll get it." Bonnie pulled the cord again. Then again and again, as fast as she could. The motor didn't start.

The dino-reptile-whale-thing swam a leisurely circle around the boat.

"Bonnie," Lori said.

"Hold on."

The creature dived.

Bonnie pulled the starter cord. The motor coughed, then died.

"Is it out of gas?"

"Don't know, ain't my boat." Bonnie kept pulling the cord.

Greg twisted in her arm, and she clutched him more tightly. Zane held her and trembled.

There was a moment of silence. Then with a crack and a brilliant flash of lightning, the storm opened up its full fury. In a moment Lori felt like she had stepped into the shower and turned the cold water up as far as it would go.

Rain splashed against the water already pooled in the bottom of the boat.

Lori hoisted Zane over her shoulder. She held onto Greg as tightly as she could. "Can't get any wetter," she said.

"What?" Bonnie said. "No, you ain't gonna—"

Lori kissed each of her sons on his head, pulled them tightly against her body, and jumped. They hit the water with jarring force. It was cold, but no colder than the rain. Behind her, the boat exploded upward , the sea creature pushing the craft into the sky as it tried to swallow it whole.

Underwater, she kicked up. She pushed the boys toward air. She fought to find the surface between surging waves.

They finally emerged and gasped for air.

The reptilian behemoth threw its head back and forth nearby, making more waves. She saw a large piece of the boat in its toothy maw, seemingly stuck there. The monster gagged on it.

It dived.

"Bonnie!" Lori shouted. No response.

I'm sorry I abandoned you, she thought, *but I had to save my boys.*

She turned toward the building. She had to get them out of the water before some other monster showed up.

It was hard to swim without using her arms. She flipped onto her back and kicked and kicked to keep all three heads out of the water. Still it washed over them with every wave.

Something bumped her leg. A fish? A shark? Something

worse? She gasped and tried to pull away. The object became visible as it floated to the surface.

A person. No, *part* of one. Enough left to recognize her as Amanda Hotchkiss, a sweet, shy young lady who came to Lady's Poker every week and never won.

Lori kicked away from the partial body. Zane and Greg were too busy coughing and blinking water out of their eyes to see. She was grateful for that.

Her back hit something. It was hard, but it didn't bite or pull her under. She turned and found a computer desk bobbing on the water.

Not letting go of the boys, Lori touched the desk. It moved with the waves, one side up, then the other. It wasn't a very stable platform, but it would get the kids out of the water, she hoped.

"Zane, honey," she said.

"Wha—" He coughed and opened one eye.

"I need you to climb up a little."

"Don't want to."

"It's important."

"No!" He clung to her fiercely.

"Please, honey. Mommy can't swim like this much longer."

Zane lifted his head and looked at the bobbing desk. He let go of Lori's neck.

"Good boy," she said. She helped him up onto the wooden surface. It wasn't easy, any weight on one side tilt up. "Sit in the middle," she told him.

When he was almost centered on the desk, Lori pushed Greg up onto it. "Hold him," she said. Zane put his arms around his brother and pulled him close.

Getting herself onto the desk seemed impossible. It tilted too easily, as well as riding the waves up and down. She decided she needed to be the motor for this little craft anyway.

The tower was closer, about three stories out of ten above the water, its antenna going up another thirty feet or so. She could make it. She had to. She started pushing the desk toward the tower, using her legs for propulsion, trying not to think about what kinds of horrors might be swimming below.

At least the rain had let up a little. The thunder receded into the distance, muttering softly. Lori looked up every minute or two to make sure she was still going the right direction.

"Mommy," she heard Zane say.

What now?

"Mommy. Mommy. Mommy."

"Little busy here, honey." She looked at him. He pointed out over the water.

"The lady."

She twisted her head but couldn't see anyone. Then she heard a cheery call. "Hey y'all!"

"Bonnie!" Lori shouted. "Where are you?"

In a moment, Bonnie swam up to the desk and put a hand on it. Her hair was a mess and her makeup washed off, but it looked like she was in one piece.

"Look!" she said. "People. And Kenny is there!"

Lori looked where Bonnie pointed. Behind the glass windows, on the floor just above the water, a group of people stared out at them. Finally, help.

A fish popped out of the water. Silver, and very large. It looked like the kind of catch a proud fisherman might have mounted on a plaque. It had a blunt mouth full of teeth and an ugly bump on its head.

The fish latched onto Bonnie's uplifted arm and pulled it down as it splashed back into the water.

Bonnie screamed.

Zane burst into hysterics as Bonnie disappeared under the water.

Lori dived down, letting go of the computer desk. Bonnie was still within reach. Her eyes were wide, and a silent scream bubbled out of her mouth. Lori grabbed the woman's free arm and tried to pull her away from the fish.

The air in Lori's lungs started to run out. She needed to resurface, to breathe, but the fish pulled Bonnie farther and farther down.

Something moved through the water beside her.

Another fish?

No. A man.

He swam down past her, holding something in his hand.

More blood, lots of it, flowed up toward the surface. The downward pull stopped. Lori kicked toward air, and life. She pulled on Bonnie and sensed the man nearby doing the same.

Air was sweet. She took it in. Other heads popped out of the water next to her. Bonnie with her eyes closed. And another.

"Kenny?" Lori said.

She heard a call of "Mommyyy!" The computer desk. The kids. She turned in the water, desperately trying to see them, but all she saw was water and the scientists in the window.

"They'll be okay," Kenny said. "We'll get them." He had a big kitchen knife in one hand. A strip of scaly fish skin dangled from the blade.

Lori turned Bonnie and looked at her bitten arm. It was shredded below the elbow.

"Stop the bleeding," she said. "Tie something around her arm."

Kenny nodded. He squirmed in the water and produced his belt. He tied it around his grandmother's arm and pulled it tight. Not tight enough, probably, but sufficient for the time being.

"Let's get out of the water."

Kenny pulled Bonnie toward the tower. Lori saw that one of the big glass windows was now broken. Several of the scientists stood behind it looking out.

"Mommyyyyyyyyyyyyyyyyyyyyyy!"

Which way? Where were they?

Then Zane's voice: "Daddy!"

Where was he? She saw him, swimming and pushing the computer desk toward the tower. When he got to the window, scientists kneeled and pulled the two boys into the building.

Lori almost fainted with relief. She had really done it, really saved her kids.

She swam toward the tower. Steve met her in the water. With a splash, they came together in a hug, then a kiss.

He said, "Let's get into the building."

The scientists who helped Lori, Steve, and Kenny up into the tower, clearly had their own stories to tell. Most of them had scratches or wounds. Some of them were armed with guns or knives or makeshift clubs.

Kenny knelt nearby, tending to his grandmother. Some of the others helped, trying to make her comfortable. She didn't look good.

Lori checked on Zane and Greg. Both were shivering.

"Are there any blankets or anything?"

"Here," a man she didn't know said. He took off his suit jacket and gave it to her. She put it on Zane. Someone else provided a sweater to wrap Greg in.

She needed to change him out of his soaked diaper.

She turned to the group. "What the hell did you do?"

The group looked blank.

"A sea in the desert?" she prompted. "Dinosaurs?"

Steve started to say something.

"We can't tell her about our work," hissed a short man with thick glasses.

Steve said, "Do you still think we have *jobs*, Carl?"

Carl shut up.

"It's the Narobrian Sea," piped up a man with a bushy mustache.

"Huh?"

"The Great Inland Sea that covered a lot of North America during the Cretaceous."

"It's a time bubble," Steve said.

Lori looked at him.

"The theory was that a time bubble could be formed in a fusion reactor bombarded with enough neutrinos, and—"

"We've been making time bubbles for months," the mustached man said. "Today we tried to expand one. It...well, it worked. But the neutrinos—"

"Forget the physics," Lori said. "It doesn't matter. Tell me *why*."

"Collins," Steve said.

Walter Collins, who founded Collins Research Ltd. The press called him a reclusive billionaire, but he had appeared at a company dinner not long after she, Steve, and the boys moved to town. He was a silver haired man in his seventies, still in good shape. Lori had shaken his hand.

"He started all this for one reason," Steve continued. "To send a message."

"A text message," another man chimed in. Lori recognized him. Bernie, the team's computer expert. She'd talked to him for half an hour at the company dinner. "The first text message sent back in time."

"Steve, honey," Lori said, "you all sound like lunatics."

"I know." He waved his hands apologetically. "But it's true. The message he wants to send is 'Darling, please take the car this morning.'"

"Mrs. Collins died in a commuter train crash six years ago," another man said.

Lori couldn't take it all in. "The whole thing," she said. "The company, the town, the secrecy, were all so Collins could tell his wife not to take the train."

"Yeah," Steve said.

"Can you fix it?"

"Fix—"

"Turn it off, make it right, put everything back to normal."

"We can turn off the reactor," Steve said. "But we don't know what will happen. We might be stuck in the Cretaceous permanently."

"Or we might bounce back to our time," Bernie said, "but—"

"I doubt it will be normal, like it was," Steve finished. "We just don't know."

"And you haven't turned it off yet, because..." Lori said.

"Collins has locked us out of the computer," Bernie said.

"We had to fight his security force just to get up here," Steve said.

Bernie looked at the pistol in his good hand and then at a smear of blood on his shirt. He said nothing.

Lori clenched her jaw. "Where is he?"

"Collins?" Steve said. "He locked himself in his office."

"Show me," she told Bernie. "Steve, watch the kids. Greg needs to be changed."

Bernie glanced at Steve, who shrugged.

Bernie led her up a flight of stairs to the top floor of the tower.

He stopped in an area with a reception desk and a heavy wooden door and said, "It's a security door, steel behind the wood. No way to break in. We tried to reason with Collins. He can see us and hear us." He pointed to a security camera over the door. "But he won't listen."

Lori said. "Stay out of sight." Bernie looked confused, but went into the hall. She knocked on the door. "Mr. Collins?"

"Who are you?" Collins' voice came over a speaker.

"Lori Barnes, Mr. Collins. We met at the dinner a couple of years ago."

"I told them all I won't shut it down. It's too important."

"I understand. You just want to save her."

There was a pause. "They weren't supposed to tell anyone," the speaker said.

"Does secrecy matter now? What you need is a way to get your wife back."

"Yes, I—"

"You really love her."

"Yes." Collins sounded teary, which was exactly what she wanted.

"I think I can help."

"You? How?"

"You've been trying to do this with science, but I have another way."

Silence over the speaker.

"Sometimes I can talk to them," Lori said, pulling this out of years of TV watching. "The ones that have passed on."

"Nonsense," Collins said.

"How much has it all cost you?" she asked. "Can it hurt to try something that's free?"

"Just you," the speaker said. Lori nodded at the camera.

After a long pause, the door clicked open.

I can't believe that worked.

Lori grabbed the door's edge and shouted, "Bernie!"

Bernie ran into the office, followed by some of the scientists.

"No!" Collins screamed. She hurried into the office, an old-fashioned, wood-paneled room with a large desk.

"You conniving bitch!" Collins said as she walked toward him.

He had aged since she last saw him. His hair was thinner and more white than silver.

"You egotistical, selfish, stupid asshole," Lori said. She turned to Bernie. "May I borrow that?" She took the pistol and turned to Collins.

"You're going to give Bernie here the computer password," she said and thumbed off the safety.

Collins cowered in his chair. "This was the only way. My only chance."

"No. This was lunacy. And it almost cost me everything." She pointed the gun at his forehead.

"I had to try."

She pulled back the hammer. "Computer code. Now."

"We could work something out. I can pay you anything."

Lori moved the gun a little to the side and fired into the floor. It was very loud.

"Rhondasboobs," Collins said.

"What?"

"That's my password."

Bernie snorted. "We tried everything with his wife's name. We never thought of that." He sat down at Collins' desk and punched the code into the computer keyboard.

After a moment, he said, "I'm in."

Lori pressed the pistol against Collins' forehead.

"Lori, honey," Steve put his hand on her shoulder. She didn't know when he'd come in. "Don't do this."

Lori kept her eye on Collins. "Do we need him any more?"

"No. We're ready," Bernie said.

"But," Steve said, "you can't just shoot him."

Lori thought of the thousands of spouses and children in the town of Collins, drowned in a prehistoric sea. The last two hours of panic and danger, the body of Amanda

Hotchkiss, and Bonnie lying bleeding downstairs. She thought of how many times her children almost died.

There was one family member who hadn't made it. He was small and barked in the middle of the night and sometimes piddled on the floor, but he was family. Grief and rage filled her.

"Hit it, Bernie," Lori said. Then she looked Collins right in the eye.

"This is for Fuffy," she said and pulled the trigger.

ACKNOWLEDGEMENTS

Many people helped me put this anthology together, and for that I'm very grateful—you wouldn't be reading this now if it weren't for them—but I'd like to give special thanks to the following three gentlemen: Robert Duperre, Enoch Pyle, and Jonathan Herron. You guys are, by all accounts, gods among men. I'd also like to thank my wife and daughters. They supported me—as always—and bore with me when they had to sacrifice family time so I could slave away at the computer. I don't think a busy husband and daddy can ask much more than that.

DP

ABOUT THE AUTHORS

ROBERT J. DUPERRE is a lover of literature in all its forms. Be it horror, fantasy, science fiction, literary fiction, or even romance, he delves into it all and relishes every minute of it. It is his desire to show this love of all genres by creating wide-reaching stories that defy classification, that can reach the widest possible audience.

Robert lives in northern Connecticut with his wife, the artist Jessica Torrant, his three wonderful children, and Leonardo the one-eyed wonder yellow Lab. Visit www.theriftonline.com for more information.

With more than 200,000 books sold, SCOTT NICHOLSON has written supernatural, thriller, and fantasy novels, comic books, screenplays, children's books, and poetry. His *Fear* series is published by Amazon's Thomas & Mercer imprint. Follow "hauntedcomputer" on Twitter and Facebook, or visit Nicholson's website at www.hauntedcomputer.com.

RUTH FRANCISCO worked in the film industry for fifteen years before selling her first novel *Confessions of a Deathmaiden* to Warner Books in 2003, followed by *Good Morning, Darkness*, which was selected by *Publishers Weekly* as one of the best mysteries of the year, and her controversial third novel, *The Secret Memoirs of Jacqueline Kennedy Onassis*. She now has four new mystery/thrillers, including the popular *Amsterdam 2012*, up on Kindle. She is a frequent contributor to *The Ellery Queen Mystery Magazine* and currently lives in Florida.

WILLIAM MEIKLE is a Scottish writer with ten novels published in the genre press and over 200 short story credits in thirteen countries. He is the author of the ongoing *Midnight Eye* series among others, and his work appears in a number of professional anthologies. His ebook *The Invasion* has been as high as #2 in the Kindle SF charts. He lives in a remote corner of Newfoundland with icebergs, whales and bald eagles for company. In the winters he gets warm vicariously through the lives of others in cyberspace, so please check him out at www.williammeikle.com.

DANIEL PYLE is the author of *Dismember*, *Down the Drain*, *Freeze*, the upcoming *Man vs. Himself*, and many short stories. He is also the editor of *Unnatural Disasters* and an Active member of the Horror Writers Association. After studying creative writing at Amherst College, he moved back to his hometown of Springfield, Missouri, where he now lives with his wife and two daughters. You can visit him online at www.danielpyle.com.

KEITH GOUVEIA lives in Florida with his wife, Lisa. He is a mechanical engineer by trade and writes fiction in his spare time. He has had work accepted for publication in numerous forthcoming anthologies, and if you're looking for something frightening, he recommends his zombie novellas, *Death Puppet: Revolt of the Dead* and *The Black Cat and The Ghoul* co-written with Edgar Allan Poe, or his collection of werewolf tales, *Animal Behavior And Other Tales Of Lycanthropy*, but if fantasy is what you crave, then check out his YA novel, *Children Of The Dragon*, all four titles published by Coscom Entertainment, or either one of his novellas, *A Storm To Remember* or *Behind The Stained Glass*, available now. And be on the lookout for his next release, *The Goblin Princess*, to be released by The Little Library of Fantasy.

Born and raised in Corona California, DANIELLE BOURDON has been dreaming up stories since she was 11. Her first two novels, *Dréoteth* and *Bound by Blood*, were published in 2010. She has already written a third novel, *Sin and Sacrifice*, published in June 2011. The sequel is due out late fall of the same year. Her love of the thriller and horror genre prompted her to write a collection of short horror stories titled *Cemetery Psalms* and a *Zombie Kids* short story series, both available in January, 2011.

Danielle lives in Texas with her husband, two sons and black cat Sheba. Visit her website for updates and contests: www.daniellebourdon.com.

J.A. TITUS currently resides in Taunton, MA, with her husband, three young children, and German shepherd pup named Deuce. She is the author of *The Kindness of Strangers* (2010), and is currently working on three WIPs: *The Last Curl*, *From Heaven*, and a short horror story collection to be released under her pseudonym, Spencer Collins. She is also a contributor to *With Love...indie writers united* (2011) and *Unnatural Disasters* (2011).

ROBIN MORRIS is the author of a number of short stories, collected in *Halloween Sky and Other Nightmares*, and one novel, *Mama*. She grew up in a nice, normal home and this made her bitter and twisted. She has lurked in several states, on both coasts of the U.S. and in the middle of the country. Currently dwelling in the Los Angeles area, Robin can be seen plotting stories of murder and mayhem in her head while working at various low-level, low-paying jobs. She dreams of the day she can spend more time writing than driving a bus.